A Hand-Me-Down Heart

Texas General Cozy Cases
Of Romance
Book 1

BECKI WILLIS

Cover Design by Anelia Savova (annrsdesign.com)

Editing by Susan Soares (SJS Editorial Services)

ISBN: 978-0-9987902-5-1

OTHER BOOKS BY BECKI

Forgotten Boxes
Plain Roots
Tangible Spirits
He Kills Me, He Kills Me Not
Mirrors Don't Lie Series
     The Girl from Her Mirror – Book 1
     Mirror, Mirror on Her Wall – Book 2
     Light from Her Mirror – Book 3
The Sisters, Texas Mystery Series
     Chicken Scratch – Book 1
     When the Stars Fall – Book 2
     Stipulations & Complications – Book 3
     Home Again: Starting Over – Book 4
     Genny's Ballad – Book 5
     Christmas In The Sisters – Book 6
     The Lilac Code – Book 7
     Wildflower Wedding (With a Killer Reception) – Book 8
     Sitting On a Fortune – Book 9
Spirits of Texas Cozy Mystery Series
     Inn the Spirit of Legends – Book 1
     Inn the Spirit of Trickery – Book 2
Texas General Cozy Cases
     A Case of Murder by Monte Carlo-Book 1

CONTENTS

ACKNOWLEDGMENTS   i
CHAPTER ONE   1
CHAPTER TWO   12
CHAPTER THREE   23
CHAPTER FOUR   34
CHAPTER FIVE   46
CHAPTER SIX   57
CHAPTER SEVEN   65
CHAPTER EIGHT   77
CHAPTER NINE   87
CHAPTER TEN   99
CHAPTER ELEVEN   114
CHAPTER TWELVE   124
ABOUT THE AUTHOR   142

ACKNOWLEDGMENTS

This book is dedicated to the many heroes who faithfully serve in our Armed Forces. A special note of appreciation goes to my son-in-law, Staff Sgt. Jerry Adams, for his service and sacrifice.

CHAPTER ONE

The tang of antiseptic hung in the air, accented with notes of coffee, bleach, and the unmistakable scent of blood.

Funny, how a girl could actually miss those smells!

With an amused smile, Grace Stavenaugh swiped her nurse's badge and declared herself back on duty.

She greeted her co-worker with cheer. "Good morning!"

Shanae Burns turned with a responding smile. "Hey, girl. How were your days off? Did you get moved into your new condo?"

"Yes. And I'm loving it! It was exactly the change I needed."

"That's awesome, girl. I'm happy for you."

"Thanks, Shanae." It was no secret that Grace had recently gone through some difficult times. Her friends and coworkers were all rooting for her to bounce back to her usual buoyant self. "How's the floor looking?"

"I'd say over half the beds are full," Shanae guesstimated, visualizing *Texas General's* second floor Med-Surg wing. "Probably one or two of the same patients that were here last week."

"What about Dierra, that sweet girl who was in the car accident? Several broken bones, ruptured spleen, concussion. Is she still here?"

"Yes, but she's made remarkable improvement. I hope she's able to go home in a day or so."

Grace pulled her long blond strands into a thick ponytail, securing it with a colorful tie. "Me, too. What about Mr. Samuelson, the guy with unexplained breathing difficulty?"

"He went home Saturday. Turns out his granddaughters live with him, and they were collecting pretty yellow flowers from the roadside to decorate their bedroom." Shanae's dark eyes danced with humor.

"Let me guess. Good old Texas weeds?"

"Bingo. And Mr. Samuelson is highly allergic."

"You gotta love a simple solution." Grace grinned.

"Yes, and I have a simple solution for my exhaustion. Eight, uninterrupted hours of blissful sleep in my own bed." The night-shift nurse gave a mock salute. "Nurse Burns, signing out. I leave the floor to you, my friend."

"Be safe driving home."

Shanae started to turn away but stopped to add, "Oh, I just remembered. Doctor Renaldi is doing some sort of experimental testing this week. A guy just checked into 214. He'll be here for several days. Best of all, he's a real hottie." Her eyebrows wiggled in suggestion.

Grace frowned. "You know I'm not in the market for a boyfriend."

"Doesn't hurt to look, now does it?"

Choosing to ignore the jibe, Grace concentrated on the medical aspect of the new patient. "What sort of experimental testing?"

"They were in Iraq together. Something about the

long-term effects of war, physically, mentally, and emotionally. Dr. Renaldi is conducting a study on it. From what I understand, that was one of the conditions of his contract. He'd only come to *Texas General* if they agreed to further his study."

"Sounds interesting."

Shanae grinned. "The test or the hot guy?"

Grace's tone left no room for doubt. "The test."

Waving goodbye to her departing friend, Grace padded down the hallway to the nurse's station, deliberately ignoring the open door to Room 214. Her life was much too busy right now to think about hot guys and boyfriends, or the lack thereof. At twenty-six, she was in no hurry to rush into a romantic relationship. One disastrous attempt was enough for her, thank you very much.

Having a famous older sister was one thing. Grace was accustomed to living just outside the spotlight. In fact, she was quite comfortable existing within the shadows. It had been that way their entire lives; Hope was the talented one, and Grace was the studious one. Hope excelled in music and dance competitions; Grace excelled in academics. If the truth were known, rather than envying her sister's fame and notoriety, Grace couldn't help but feel sorry for her. Long ago, Hope had sacrificed privacy for the sake of stardom. It suited Grace that most people were too dazzled with her sister to notice her there in the shadows.

As a child, she hadn't even minded being dragged along to all of Hope's auditions and performances. Her sister was an amazing violinist, and her talent had taken the entire family on fabulous vacations as they chased from one venue to another. Even dance competitions— their father's stab at giving his daughter a normal teenage experience—had been fun in their own way. Within the pages of a good book, Grace traveled far and wide while sitting on the sideline.

And there was no doubt that Grace benefited from her sister's extensive wardrobe, even though some of the hand-me-downs weren't her style. Her only sibling had a passion for the latest trends and designer tags. The styles looked great on Hope, but the clothes had always looked different on her, even though the two shared the same tall, willowy build. Grace suspected it had more to do with the attitude and confidence of the person wearing them than it did the clothes. Hope preferred high heels and plunging necklines. Grace was most comfortable in jeans and a cotton shirt. Scrubs suited her best of all.

Grace loved her sister, and she held no ill will toward her dominance in their lives. Fair or not, the Stavenaugh household had revolved around Hope. Grace had no doubt their parents would have done the same for her, had she shown similar talent and passion for any particular skill. But Grace's dream had always been a career in nursing, and how did you prep a child for that? Her parents had encouraged her, certainly. They had taken her to various college campuses and helped her select the best schools and courses, and they had provided the funds for her master's degree. Still, it was little comparison to the time, effort, and money invested in Hope's career. There were no weekends on the road, attending competitions for administering painless IVs or perfect bandaging. No private tutors or expensive instruments. Certainly, there were no grand auditoriums, filled with hushed audiences left stunned and breathless after a brilliant performance of restraining a patient. No, the dream chasing had all been dedicated to Hope.

It was one thing to bow to her sister when they were

children, but it was quite another now that they were adults. Grace drew the line when it came to the things closest to her soul: her love life and her career. Those, she wasn't sharing with her sister.

Too bad, I didn't realize that was Julian's angle until after *I fell for him!* Grace chided herself. Her brow gathered into a sulk. *With a name like Julian, I should have known he had musical ambitions. He was only using me to get close to Hope and to further his own career. What a jerk. And what an idiot I was for believing him. That one's on you, Gracie girl.*

Putting aside thoughts of Julian and men in general, Grace logged onto the computer at the nurse's station.

"Grace, you're back!"

"I was only off four days," she reminded her friend, Cami St. John.

"I know, but I missed you. As did all your patients." Cami perched on the edge of the desk. "So? How did it go?"

"I'm all moved, but it wasn't nearly enough time to get everything organized."

"But you like your new place?"

"It's perfect! Exactly what I was looking for."

"Awesome. When my lease comes up for renewal, I may check on a vacancy there."

"Give me time to get organized, and I'll invite you and Randy for dinner."

"Just me, if you don't mind. We broke up."

"Oh? I'm sorry to hear that."

"I'm not," Cami said with an honest smile. "I'm not sure what took us so long. After dating for so long, I guess we just didn't want to admit we'd grown apart. This is definitely a good thing for both of us."

"In that case, I hear there's a good-looking guy in 214." It may not have been fair, but Grace tried Shanae's

5

matchmaking tactics on Cami.

"Oh, he's more than good-looking!" Cami assured her. Pushing herself up from the desk, she added, "Unfortunately, he's your patient. And that buzzer going off is mine, so I guess I'll start my morning there."

Grace took a cue from her friend and started her own rounds. There was a post-surgical patient who needed wound care and another whose IV had backed up. Over a half hour later, Grace made her way to Dierra's room. She had bonded with the teenager before her days off, and while she hated to see the girl still suffering, Grace was happy to visit with her again.

She couldn't say exactly why—perhaps stubbornness on her own part—Grace put off visiting Room 214. She bypassed the room to tend to a patient on the other side, saving that room for last. Finally, she knocked on the open door and asked to come in.

"Come in," a gravelly voice responded.

"Hello," she said, using her standard smile as she approached the man in the bed. His dark head was bent as he read from a hardcover book. "I'm Grace, and I'll be your nurse for the next few days. I understand you'll be with us for most of the week."

"That's what they tell me," the man said. He took his time slipping a bookmark between the pages and closing the covers.

A jolt of familiarity slammed through Grace when she saw his face. He looked like an older, more mature, more battered version of her first major crush. But that was crazy. This hardened, rigid-looking man couldn't be—

"Cruz? Cruz Colton, is that you?" she gasped.

"Grace Stavenaugh." His wasn't a question. Nor was his raspy voice particularly friendly.

"I, uh, had no idea you were back in the Brazos

Valley," Grace stuttered, trying to recover from her surprise. In her wildest dreams, she never expected to see him here, in her hospital. And she certainly never expected him to look so unhappy about it.

His cool demeanor stung more than she expected. She wasn't foolish enough to think he had returned her feelings, but she thought they had at least been friends.

"I'm not back," he pointed out. "Not permanently. I'm just here to help Doc with his study."

Grace looked down at the chart she held. "You're a combat soldier?"

"Not anymore." There was a wealth of unspoken commentary in his sigh.

"I had no idea," Grace murmured. She had lost contact with him once he graduated, two years before her. A note of respect moved into her voice as she looked him squarely in the eye and softly said, "I thank you for your service."

Something flickered in Cruz's dark eyes. His nostrils flared slightly, proof that her appreciation and admiration affected him more than he cared to show. His hard stare softening the tiniest of bits, he said, "It was an honor serving my country."

"I understand you and Doctor Renaldi were both in Iraq. Is that where you met him?"

"Yes. We became friends and stayed in contact, even after he came back stateside."

"You didn't?" she guessed.

"Not right away." His simple answer made it clear the subject was closed.

"So, what do you do now? Where do you live?" Grace asked the questions in a friendly voice, sensing his need for privacy. She started taking his vitals and recorded her findings. Her mind raced, right along with her heart.

Play it cool, Gracie girl. Don't make a fool of yourself in front of him. Been there, done that. Time to move along.

Unaware of the pep talk taking place in her head, Cruz answered the question on a rueful note. "I haven't decided yet."

Grace's distracted mind scrambled to keep up. "About which question?" Her lips curved in a slight smile; surely, the man knew where he lived!

He wasn't smiling. "Both." Seeing the look that flooded into her eyes, he quickly set the record straight. "I'm not homeless!" Cruz practically barked. "I just haven't settled yet."

"Of course. I understand."

"Do you?" His voice came out sharp.

Compassion softened her face. "I think so. You've been busy defending our country, living on foreign ground, moving from base to base even on home soil. I would imagine it doesn't leave much time for establishing roots." She unwound the blood pressure cuff from his arm, noting the thick cord of muscle and the inked images upon them. An elaborate tattoo touted his love of the United States and his home state of Texas. Two flags, one from each domain, wound around an eagle bearing arms and the words 'Freedom Ain't Free.'

A sigh escaped his lips as Cruz reached up to scrub the back of his neck. His reply had come out more intense than he intended. It wasn't her fault that he was still raw over his recent discharge from the Army. After ten years of being in charge of not only his own fate but the lives and safety of the countless people they protected, now that he was back in civilian life, he felt suddenly adrift. He had chosen not to take the commission offered by top officials, but there were times, like now, when Cruz wondered about the wisdom of that choice.

"Look. The thing is… I didn't mean—"

Grace interrupted him before he could blunder his way through an apology. "I'm sure you didn't. I see here you're scheduled for a sonogram and an echocardiogram." She consulted her watch. "As a matter of fact, in just about fifteen minutes."

"Doc has a full itinerary for me."

"Can I get you anything? Another blanket? More pillows?"

"Since a fat, juicy steak and a baked potato are out of the question, I guess not."

"Yeah, sorry about that. Not happening."

Cruz tilted his head, studying her with his dark gaze. The frost had thawed, but his eyes were still guarded. "You've changed since I saw you last."

Grace sputtered out a short laugh. "I should hope so! That was at least ten years ago. I was, like, sixteen. A gawky teenager." She cringed at the memory, thinking of how plain and awkward she must have looked next to her glamorous older sister.

"You were never gawky."

His solemn voice, now so much deeper and more resonating than she remembered, conspired with his unreadable eyes to send a shiver racing across her skin. Grace refused to identify the source of the shiver, afraid it might very well be delight. She couldn't go down that path again. Even without the baggage of the past between them, Cruz had too many demons in his closeted stare. Grace was trying hard to simplify her life, not complicate it more.

Forcing herself to focus on that old baggage, she asked in a superficially sweet voice, "Do you ever hear from Hope?"

If she thought his eyes were closeted before, she saw a door slam now. "Now, why would I hear from your sister?" he all but growled.

Grace lamely lifted one shoulder. "I thought you may have kept in touch."

"I was never in touch with Hope." His voice was flat.

Beneath her breath, so low that he barely heard the words, Grace muttered, "Was anyone?" When she spoke up in a louder voice, there was an unmistakable ring of pride in her voice. No matter what else had transpired between the sisters, Grace loved her sibling and was proud of her accomplishments. "I'm sure you've followed her career. Hope is an accomplished violinist. Her concerts draw masses, filling the largest of concert halls."

"Did she ever play overseas?"

"Several times in Western Europe. She's played the finest halls in Great Britain, France, Italy, and Germany."

"But not the Middle East?" he asked pointedly. "Not a USO tour?"

"No," Grace admitted.

"I prefer Toby Keith, Luke Bryan, and Craig Morgan. You know. Guys who support the troops."

"Chauvinistic, much?" she mused lightly.

Cruz held her gaze. "If she'd shown us the respect of coming to play for us, we would have shown her the respect of attending. Even if we didn't like the music."

Grace had no input in her sister's career and couldn't begin to make excuses for her. Knowing Hope, her reasons for not performing on bases had stemmed more from a dislike of sand and spiders than from lack of support for American troops. But she couldn't say that. Instead, Grace offered a smile. "The guys would have loved her show. She does something totally unique, blending her love of dance routines with her talents on the violin. It's quite something."

"It's not too late," Cruz pointed out his voice still sharp. "Just because I'm back doesn't mean there aren't thousands of troops still there, begging for a taste of home. Craving anything American, anything current."

Grace found she couldn't hold his intense gaze. "I'll—I'll be sure and pass that on to her manager."

"Is that how you have to talk to your own sister now? Through her manager?" His tone was incredulous and more than just a touch condescending.

"No, of course not!" Never mind that it sometimes came down to that. Hope was terrible about checking and returning messages.

Grace was thankful the aides arrived at that exact moment to take him for tests. It saved her from more of this awkward conversation. She concentrated on helping unhook monitors and straighten covers.

As they rolled him to the door, Cruz cast a glance her way. "Let the fun begin."

"Oh, no," Grace said, unable to resist an impish smile. "That starts this afternoon. You have a colonoscopy scheduled for first thing tomorrow morning."

CHAPTER TWO

Cruz wore a scowl as the aides wheeled him out for tests. Why had he been so hostile toward Grace, of all people? She was the sweetest, kindest girl he had ever known.

At least, he acknowledged, the teenage version of her had been that way, but he doubted much had changed. If anything, he imagined those traits had only intensified. Even teens that were completely self-centered and obnoxious often mellowed into decent human beings; Cruz seldom heard of the opposite happening. No, he instinctively knew that Grace was still gentle and kind, and yet he had treated her as if she were the enemy.

Hope, on the other hand, was a different story. He harbored no disillusions about the older Stavenaugh sibling growing up to be a kind, generous, decent adult. Some apples were rotten to the core, and Hope definitely fell in that category.

He didn't lie when he said he hadn't been in touch with Hope. He hadn't, neither emotionally, physically, nor verbally. That didn't mean, however, that she hadn't tried reaching out to him. She had called on two

12

occasions, both ironically after a stir in the media that painted Cruz as a hero. He supposed Grace hadn't been aware of his fleeting fifteen minutes of fame, and that suited him fine. Not so, her sister. Hope faithfully followed the gossip pages and all social media connections, no doubt hoping to see her own name in the news. At the first hint of rising stardom, Hope looked for a way to hitch her star to his.

The first time, Cruz had taken her call. The second time, he let it go unanswered. Clearly, some people never changed. And even more clearly, Hope was nothing like her younger sister.

Which brought him back to his current dilemma. How many times had he thought of Grace's sweet smile while he was on a mission? How often had he fantasized about her and what might have been? Many a cold, lonely night in the desert, he had stayed warm by replaying every conversation they ever had, by recalling the sound of her twinkling laughter and the light in her hazel eyes. She didn't possess the kind of staggering beauty her sister had, but in its own quiet way, Grace's beauty was even more stunning, because it went straight through to her soul.

Cruz admitted he had handled seeing her again completely wrong. Earlier that morning, he had caught a glimpse of a woman—obviously Grace— who reminded him of his high school crush. It brought back a wealth of unwanted feelings and memories. He didn't want to relive that time in his life, and the way one single, ruined evening had set the course for his future. Too much had happened that night. It had changed his life forever, and, in a roundabout way, that night was the reason he was here now, undergoing tests for his buddy's medical study.

Joe Renaldi, known affectionately to his friends simply as Doc, had saved Cruz's life. Not only that, Doc had saved his leg, and for those two deeds, Cruz was eternally grateful. If he spent one or two weeks a year letting his friend poke and prod him, taking pictures from the inside out and turning him into a human guinea pig to further his point that war was hazardous to one's health, then so be it. Cruz did so without reservation and without pay. It was the least he could do.

It wasn't Grace's fault that he was between a rock and a hard place. It hurt too much to think about the past, and the future wasn't looking too promising, either. Until he could work it out in his own head, he needed to steer clear of the one woman he didn't want to hurt.

Avoiding his primary nurse was easier said than done.

"And here we are!" Grace appeared at his door around the noon hour, a tray in her hand and a bright smile on her lovely face. Cruz tried hard not to notice. "One yummy liquid lunch, for your dining pleasure."

He sat in the chair beside the bed, a surprisingly comfortable model that swiveled and reclined. With an economy of motion, Grace slipped a nearby table across his lap and deposited the tray with a flourish.

She smelled like lemons and sunshine. That, too, he tried not to notice.

Perusing the offering, his mouth turned downward. "I thought you said yummy."

"It is," she insisted, her hazel eyes dancing with laughter. "*If* you like weak chicken broth, lemon Jell-O, lime Jell-O, white grape juice, black coffee, and tea. *Bon appetit.*"

"Easy for you to say," he grunted.

"Don't worry. For dessert, I'm bringing you a delicious cocktail of pills and laxatives."

"Joy." His wry tone expressed anything but.

"All in the name of science, right?"

"Absolutely. I wouldn't do this otherwise, but I owe my life to Doc. It's the least I can do."

The moment the words were out, Cruz wished he could take them back. He rarely spoke of his combat days, so why had he offered that piece of information so easily?

He remembered Grace always had been easy to talk to.

"Was it dangerous?" she asked softly, cocking her blond head to the side just a fraction. Just enough to let him know she was truly listening and truly interested in his reply.

"Flying into enemy territory? Not at all," he said dryly.

Her eyes widened. "You were a fighter pilot?"

Uncomfortable with the admiration shining in her hazel eyes—and far too flattered by that lovely light—he shifted in his seat and shrugged as if it weren't a big deal. "Yeah."

"Wow. I had no idea," she murmured. Her eyebrows puckered and her head cocked further to the side. "You say Doc Renaldi saved your life?"

"It was—"

Grace interrupted him; her arm extended as if she held a stop sign. "Don't you dare say it was nothing."

"Yeah, okay," he grumbled. "It was very brave and noble on his part." He looked up to glare at her, as if to say, *'happy now?'*

"And no doubt dangerous, for both of you. Did he save you medically, or physically?"

His answer was brusque. "Both."

"How awful!"

Cruz was surprised by the depth of compassion he heard in her voice. But why? Grace always had been caring and attentive. A born mender. It was no surprise she had become a nurse. Unable to downplay such concern, and not wishing to belittle Doc's heroic feat, he couldn't just toss out a glib answer.

His words were weighted and low. "I owe Doc everything."

"I can't even imagine," Grace whispered. Her eyes glittered with an array of emotions. Compassion, empathy, admiration, and pain. Afraid he might see pity, as well, Cruz looked away. It was the catalyst she needed to paste on a smile and change the subject. "I never asked. Is there a Mrs. Colton? Any little Cruz juniors running around?"

"Not a one. And no Mrs., either." He knew it was only polite to ask the same question of her, but he was afraid of the answer. Just because she didn't wear a ring while working didn't mean a thing. She wore no adornment at all, other than her bright and shining smile. He pretended interest in the watery broth as he reluctantly asked, "And you?"

"Neither. Not yet, anyway." With his eyes on the tray, he didn't see the flash of pain in her eyes, and her cheerful voice never betrayed the emotion. Taking a step backward, Grace asked, "Can I get you anything else?"

"I'll wait for the steak and baked potato."

"Maybe tomorrow," she hedged.

"I'll hold you to it."

At the door, she turned and flashed a smile. "I said *maybe*," she reminded him. "I'll be back with that dessert in a few hours. Until then, enjoy your meal."

Yeah. It would be hard to avoid his nurse.

Grace came again mid-afternoon, bringing another taste of sunshine and a paper cup filled with pills.

"Here's some apple juice to wash it all down," she offered. "And as a special treat, more of our special recipe lime Jell-O."

"You're enjoying this, aren't you?" Cruz grumbled.

"Not really. But it's a necessary evil."

He swallowed the pills at once, dry.

"How can you do that?" she asked in amazement.

"Like swallowing desert dust. Lots of practice."

She put a hand to the slender column of her own neck. "It makes my throat hurt, just watching you do that. Are you sure you don't want something to drink?"

If only to erase that look of near-horror on her face, Cruz reached for the juice carton. Their hands brushed in the process. He willed the monitor not to record the sudden uptick in his heart rate.

"Happy now?" he asked, emptying the carton in a few simple gulps.

"Yes, thank you," she replied primly.

"Anything else?" he asked sharply.

"Actually, there is. Everyone is different, but those may start to take effect soon. You may want to keep the bedpan handy, just in case." Her eyes danced in mirth, as if she enjoyed watching him squirm.

Blast it all! Cruz cringed to himself. Could it get any more embarrassing than this?

He shouldn't have asked, because he definitely did not like the answer.

A couple of hours later, he had the dream again.

Cruz zeroed in on the target below. The missile was locked and loaded. Amid the swirl of dust and the gunfire's smoky haze, it was difficult to see, but he knew the site well. An enemy camp with the technology and firepower to wreak havoc among his allies. One precisely aimed missile was all he needed to silence them forever.

Or until the next camp popped up. It wasn't a matter of if, but when.

Cruz turned to circle the camp again and get into position. That's when he saw them.

Children.

"What the—!"

His blood boiled. It was just like the enemy to bring innocent children into the war. Had they no shame?

But, of course, the answer was 'no.' They had no shame, no value of life. The enemy would use any means to fight, no matter how low and despicable the method. No matter the sacrifice, no matter the pawn.

As if to prove Cruz's theory, a man in a turban and robes came from the hut, pushing three children in front of him. He raised his rifle in the air, pumping it high in defiance, screaming some unintelligible threat to the chopper overhead.

Cruz had no choice. "Abort! Abort mission!" he commanded. He pulled up, intending to grant the camp below a temporary reprieve. A spray of gunfire hit the tail of the aircraft, and he felt it go into a spin.

It was falling, falling….

Falling.

"Cruz! Cruz, wake up." With a gentle shake, Grace stood over his bed, slowly bringing him back to reality.

Sweat drenched his entire body. Dark hair plastered against his head. His heart thundered in his chest, setting off the monitor's alarm. Cruz couldn't quite catch his breath, no matter how hard he tried. His dark eyes were wild as they turned upon her, still blinded with scenes from the past.

Not their past. *His* past. The one no woman in her right mind would want to be a part of. The one he could never burden someone else with.

"You were dreaming," she said in a soothing voice. She gently stroked his arm, using a grounding technique that slowly broke through his daze and brought him wide awake.

Gulping in greedy breaths of air, Cruz practiced a few techniques of his own. *Control. He was in control. He could do this.*

"Are you okay now?" she asked softly. Her hand remained on his arm, the pleasant weight like the cozy feel of a light blanket.

"I—I think so." He still tried to control his breathing.

"Does it happen often?" Keeping one hand on his arm and speaking in the same soft, compassionate voice, Grace twisted to reset the alarm. Already the numbers were falling, slowly returning to an acceptable range.

"Not so much anymore. But even once is too often."

"Would you like to talk about it?" she inquired softly.

He looked at her with a horrified expression. "No!" It was bad enough that she should see him like this, his soul raw and bare, his emotions stripped naked.

"It's okay, you know. And perfectly normal. Most veterans experience nightmares after returning from war. It's nothing to be ashamed of."

"Says the woman with the nice, safe, perfect life!" he snapped.

He was doing it again. He was taking his anger out on Grace. It wasn't fair, but he couldn't seem to stop himself.

One look into her wounded eyes, and he groaned in remorse. "I'm sorry," he mumbled, running his free hand over the top of his head. "That was uncalled for."

"You're right. I have a nice, safe life, thanks to men and women in uniform like you. But you're wrong about one thing. My life is far from perfect."

Perhaps because it took his mind off his own troubles, but Cruz had to ask, "What's wrong with it?"

"Believe me, it's not a quick and easy answer."

Acutely aware of the hand still upon him, Cruz's voice came out in a deep rumble. "I've got time."

She hesitated, clearly tempted to share her burdens with a man she once called her friend. Cruz wondered if she had ever thought of him as anything more, or if the attraction had all been one-sided. He'd never had the opportunity to find out. It remained one of his biggest regrets in life.

"I'll give you the condensed version," she decided. "My parents are getting a divorce, my former roommate failed to make her share of the rent payments and we lost our apartment, I've just moved—without a roommate, I might add—into an over-priced condo that I couldn't resist, my boyfriend was using me to further his musical career, I was passed over for a promotion, and Hope is coming for a visit. How's that for perfectly imperfect?"

"Wait. Your parents are getting a divorce?" He wore a stunned expression. "But… they've been married for ages! They always seemed so happy."

"I know. I'm still reeling from it all."

"I'm sorry, Grace. I really am." Cruz put his large hand over hers, his words soft and sincere. Touching her might not have been the safest of choices—for him, anyway—but his only concern right now was to comfort her. Tears welled in her beautiful hazel eyes, threatening to fall.

"So am I." He heard the heartbreak in her voice.

Cruz squeezed her hand before releasing it. She used her trembling fingers to brush the tears away.

"New condo, huh?" he asked, changing the subject to lighten the mood.

Grace nodded. "Just moved in this weekend. It's still a mess. Naturally, my sister chose this coming weekend to visit."

"I'm surprised she has a free weekend."

"She doesn't. She's playing an OPAS concert." Grace hesitated before adding, "You should go."

His grunt was answer enough, but he went on to elaborate, "With any luck, I'll either still be in here, or on my way back home."

"Which you were rather vague about," Grace reminded him. "Have you considered moving back here?"

"To Bryan-College Station?" he asked in surprise.

"Why not? You grew up here. You have friends here. Both towns have really grown since you were here last. You might be surprised at how much the twin cities have to offer now."

But looking at the woman before him, Cruz didn't need to be convinced. The area had her, and that was enticing enough.

Bad idea, dude, he reminded himself sternly.

"What about your father?" Grace went on to ask. "Does he still live here?"

"He passed away a few years ago."

"I'm sorry to hear that."

Unexpected emotions gathered in Cruz's throat when he thought about how much he still missed his dad. His father had always been his sounding board, and he still mourned the loss. Cruz could use some of his good, solid advice right about now. Unsure of what civilian life held for him, he needed his father's wisdom and quiet faith to guide him. Countless times, he had reached for the phone to call, even after all these years.

"He was a good man," Cruz agreed quietly, fighting the break in his voice.

Great. Just great. First, she sees me in the throes of a nightmare, sweating bullets and unable to breathe. Now, I'm about to blubber like a baby. What's next?

A loud rumble roared from the vicinity of his stomach, as they watched his flat belly visibly roll.

"Uh-oh," he said, eyes wide. He swung his legs over the side of the bed, not taking time to brace his scarred thigh for movement. He bolted for the bathroom, stumbling and weaving as his leg gave way but eventually held steady.

At least he saved himself from the ultimate humiliation.

CHAPTER THREE

First days back at work were always tiring. By the time her shift ended an hour later, Grace was more than ready to leave. She had been too busy moving in on her days off to go grocery shopping, and there hadn't been much to bring from her old apartment. A quick stop at *Chick-Fil-A* seemed the easiest solution.

Dropping the sack onto the kitchen counter, Grace went immediately upstairs. She needed a shower and pajama pants before eating.

Stepping into the oversized shower stall, Grace turned on all six jets. This bathroom had been the tipping point in her decision to get the condo. It was the stuff of every girl's dreams. A huge walk-in closet, accessible from both the master bath and the bedroom. A huge tiled shower with all these glorious water jets shooting out at her and a pebbled floor beneath her feet. A soaking tub. A separate commode stall, with dual lavatories set into a granite counter that went on forever. Plenty of lights, mirrors, and storage. The pièce de résistance had been the heated towel racks, and the heated floors in front of the tub and shower. The ensuite encompassed the entire second floor, with plenty of room for bedroom furniture and a small sitting area.

True, the condo was at the very tip-top of her budget. *Okay, forty dollars over,* if she was being honest. But it was worth it. Downstairs had an open concept kitchen/dining/living, with a second bedroom and a modest bathroom tucked beneath the stairs. The perfect size for just her, with room to accommodate overnight guests. Best of all, she had the corner unit, and both her patio and her upstairs balconies overlooked a wooded area, offering a taste of nature and as much privacy as one could get in a bustling college town.

Growing up, Grace and her sister never wanted for much, but their modest home didn't have luxuries like these. What extra money they had was dedicated to gas and hotel rooms, when the whole family loaded up and chased after Hope's dreams. Those non-existent nursing contests aside, equal money was never dedicated to her UIL events and academic competitions. Most often, she rode the school bus and stayed in a plain hotel room allotted to four girls at a time.

But *this.* This was like living in a luxury hotel, and Grace was determined to enjoy every moment and every amenity. Right after she turned into a prune and the hot water played out, she would go down to enjoy her fancy convection oven and her dedicated coffee bar. A decaf cappuccino would go perfectly with her chicken sandwich.

While the water sprayed at her from all angles, Grace allowed herself the added pleasure of thinking about Cruz. After all these years and all that teenage angst, it was an unexpected treat to see him again. It had taken every shred of professionalism she possessed to remain calm. Even if her inner self wanted to swoon—yes, the urge had hit her, more than once—she used remarkable self-control to appear unaffected by his sudden reappearance in her life. She wanted to believe that she hid her trembling hands well, and that her voice didn't come out sounding as breathless as it felt.

If she thought Cruz Colton was good looking as a teenager, it was nothing compared to how he looked as a man. His shoulders were wider now, thickened by age and muscle development. His entire body was lean and toned, an athletic study in sinewy strength. No wonder she found his nearness so disturbing. And his eyes! Those dark, brooding eyes had always been expressive, but new dimensions and new shadows made them so much more compelling. Cruz was more than just handsome now. With his chiseled features and intense gaze, he was commanding.

Don't even get her started on his voice. Deep and rough, but in a deliciously rugged sort of way. Grace turned into the jet's spray, trying to blast the memory of his voice from playing in her head.

The truth was, Cruz had never been far from her thoughts. How many times had she seen a tall, dark head, and thought fleetingly of her old crush? Every single time she saw or heard the name, and every time someone mentioned taking a trip on a luxury ship, her thoughts had drifted to the boy with the dark, brooding eyes and the quiet sense of humor. Cruz Colton had been her first love, even if he never knew it.

She had lost track of him after that fateful night. Perhaps it had been her pride, perhaps her attempt at self-preservation, but she had blocked him from her heart after that. Even though she had never successfully blocked him from her thoughts, she had never allowed herself to wonder what became of him. She never once tried to track him down. It was best to let bygones be bygones, and to learn from her mistakes.

Right up until the fiasco with Julian, she thought she had been successful.

The sad truth was that Cruz was another of her sister's hand-me-downs. Grace first met him when he would come over to the house, hoping to catch Hope at home and, with any luck, without a phone attached to her ear. That, of course, was back in the old days, before everyone over the age of ten had their own personal cell phone. Kids today found it hard to imagine, but the Stavenaugh girls had grown up using a landline, of all things! It wasn't always one of those monstrosities with the curly cord; that was simply the backup, when the cordless ran out of juice after hours of endless chatter. But it was a line shared by the entire family, and they were required to answer beeps. Hope monopolized the phone, just like she monopolized the bathroom the sisters shared, and their closet, and their parents' time and energy. If she was home, she was usually on the phone, but Cruz was hardly the first boy to come over and wait his turn for a morsel of Hope's attention.

It was always awkward, seeing the way those boys swarmed around her sister. They would often sit on the couch while Grace was in the living room doing her homework, having been banished from her own bedroom while Hope carried on 'a private conversation.' Grace ignored most of the waiting suitors, but there were a few, like Cruz, who were rather interesting. After a while, she looked forward to her conversations with him. He had an unfortunate knack for coming over when Hope wasn't home yet, or when she had just left the house, but Grace was more than happy to help him kill time.

It turned out the two of them had a lot in common. They had the same taste in music and movies. Both liked to read, and often discussed their current favorite author, or recommended a title for the other to read. Cruz would sometimes drop by to bring her a book, seemingly unconcerned that he had missed Hope, yet again.

Grace knew it was dangerous, getting attached to one of her sister's many admirers. They didn't normally last long. Hope's version was always that she grew bored with their infantile ways and dropped the boys like a hot potato, but Grace suspected that some simply knew when to cut their losses and move on. Cruz seemed more determined than the others, perhaps because he had yet to spend much time in Hope's presence. His timing really was awful, but he was persistent.

Deep down, Grace began to imagine that Cruz came to see *her*. That was why he never seemed concerned over missing her sister yet again, or why he often left just before Hope was due back, murmuring some lame excuse about needing to run an errand for his dad. Already completely infatuated with him, Grace spun daydreams of Cruz proclaiming his love for her and sweeping her off her feet, forsaking his former interest in her older sister. It was her own delicious fantasy, and one day soon, Grace would work up the courage to let him know how she felt. One day, she would tell him that she liked him, too. That she maybe even loved him.

Then Hope had ruined it for her. The secret fantasy, once so beautiful and pure, was suddenly tainted.

Grace would never forget that day. It was the first day her sister had broken her heart over a boy, but certainly not the last. That hadn't come until a few weeks later.

Hope had come home and found Cruz there in the living room, playing a game of cards with her younger sister. She had looked at Grace with the strangest glint in her eye, as if seeing her for the first time. It was certainly the first time she had noticed that her sixteen-year-old sister, two years her junior, had developed a figure. Hope's eyes had narrowed, as she took in the light brush of makeup and the long blond tresses, arranged casually and yet oh so attractively. Grace wore one of Hope's old outfits, a shorts set that looked surprisingly good on her little sister. The color set off her peaches and cream complexion.

Never one to stand aside and not be the focal point of a room, Hope had gone up to a very stunned Cruz and thrown her arms around him for an enthusiastic, over-the-top greeting. Grace remembered that it involved a lot of squealing and silly fawning over Cruz's strong muscles. For the next ten minutes, Hope had used every trick in her little black book of womanly wiles to wind that boy around her little finger. Not that Grace bothered to hang around and see the outcome; she fled to the bedroom, citing homework.

The telephone rang and, of course, Hope answered. A few minutes later, she appeared in the bedroom doorway.

"I have a favor to ask of you, Gracie girl."

Her sugary tone and the use of the old childhood nickname was the first warning that things were about to sour. At Grace's wary look, Hope rushed on, "Gregg just called and wants me to go to the baseball game with him. The thing is, what's his name is in the living room. If Gregg sees him here, he'll think there's something going on between us."

"I'm pretty sure Cruz—that's his name, by the way, Cruz Colton—thinks there's something going on between you, too," Grace remarked dryly. "I think it may have been the second '*why, bless your heart, look at all those muscles!*' that tipped the scale." She gave a perfect imitation of her sister's gushing voice.

"Don't be ridiculous," Hope said, brushing her comments aside. "He's nobody. He doesn't even play sports. Do me this one favor. In his own way, he is rather handsome. Think of him as a gift. Another hand-me-down to my favorite little sister."

The words had pierced Grace's tender heart, tarnishing her dreams forever. She had been a fool to think Cruz had been interested in *her*. Hope was right. He was just another of her hand-me-downs.

"I'm your only little sister," Grace had reminded her bitterly. She was still smarting, thinking that surely Cruz deserved more respect than to be tossed aside, abandoned for what her shallow sister considered a better offer. Did his feelings not matter? Was his heart so easily brushed aside? He wasn't just another of Hope's hand-me-downs. He was a wonderful, sweet, funny, intelligent young man, and Grace was suddenly the most miserable she had ever been in her life. She realized then, beyond a shadow of a doubt, that she was in love with her sister's cast off.

"That's why you're my favorite," Hope said, her blue eyes twinkling. "Do this for me, and you can keep the outfit you're wearing."

"You gave it to me last year," Grace protested, "after the second time you wore it! You said everyone had seen it already, and you'd never wear it again."

"Silly, I just loaned it to you. But it doesn't look half-bad on you. Do this, and you can keep it."

Grace would do it, but not for some stupid outfit. She would do it to save Cruz the humiliation of being there when Gregg arrived.

"Fine!" she spat, sweeping past her sister. Hope was already going through her closet, trying to decide on the most stunning outfit for an afternoon ballgame in the Texas heat.

Grace had stumbled into the living room, making up some lame excuse about Hope remembering a test she had to study for. Insisting her sister needed peace and quiet or else she might fail—something Hope would have hit the ceiling over, had she heard—Grace tugged him out the door, claiming a sudden and intense urge for Starbucks coffee. They had a new flavor, she said, and she wanted one. Right now.

She would never forget the confusion on Cruz's handsome face as he allowed her to drag him from the house, but she thought she had seen something else, too. She thought she had seen relief. Not that it mattered. Now that Hope had tagged him as a hand-me-down, Grace's innocent dreams were shattered. She would never look at Cruz Colton the same again.

Of course, she had only seen him once after that, but she couldn't dwell on that now. That trip down memory lane, that heartache, was for another day. The water already grew tepid, and she was no longer certain about the wetness on her cheeks. She couldn't tell which was from the faucet, and which was from her eyes.

She thought she was finished crying over the past. And maybe she was. She wasn't at all sure that these tears weren't for Cruz, the man, and whatever dark and bitter secrets he harbored. Grace knew a tortured soul when she saw one. Knew the telltale signs of PTSD and the nightmares that haunted a person, even during waking hours. Cruz had all that and more, and it had made him a changed man. There was an edge to him now, a hardness that hadn't been there as a youth. She knew that life and age had a way of doing that to a person, but this was so much deeper. War had fundamentally changed him. He had sacrificed so much for his country, but at what cost to him?

For that, the tears continued to pour.

Grace padded into the living room, curling up on the couch with her cappuccino. After a very thorough cry, her eyes were red and dry. Her heart still smarted.

She couldn't help but think about Cruz's response at seeing her today. Clearly, he hadn't been pleased. Was it because Hope had hurt him so deeply? Did he want to cut all ties with the girl who broke his eighteen-year-old heart, even the sister he had called his friend? Or was he embarrassed now by his own foolishness, finally able to see he had never had a chance with the flighty, self-centered Hope?

Or, her aching heart dared to realize, maybe he didn't recall their past with the same fondness she did. Just like her romantic fantasies, perhaps even the friendship had been one-sided.

A horrible thought struck her. Could it be that he, too, had used her, trying to get close to Hope?

It was that possibility which hurt most of all. Even after a decade had passed, Grace couldn't bear the thought of it. She had treasured their time together. She had considered Cruz a true and faithful friend. Any other possibility was utterly heartbreaking.

Why, then, had he been so sharp with her? True, he had mellowed by the day's end. She had even seen a glimpse of his old wry humor peeking through. Heard a hint of warmth in his voice when he spoke of his father. Felt compassion in his touch. She sensed that the old

Cruz was still in there somewhere, hidden beneath the scars and the layers of bad memories and desert dust.

A part of her ached to reach out to him. In her mind, they had once been close. She missed the boy she had known. The easy camaraderie they once shared had been strained and awkward today, but that wasn't so surprising. They hadn't seen each other in ten years. They were different people now. And, to be fair, she wasn't catching him at this best. First and foremost, they would have to get past the embarrassment he felt today when she caught him during not one, but *three* vulnerable moments.

And what was with his leg? Obviously, his wounds went deep, and some were physical. Grace itched to know the whole story, but she wasn't sure she wanted to get involved again. It had taken a long time to get over him the first time. Could she do it again?

"Who says I have to get over him?" she mused aloud, daring, for one moment, to imagine the impossible.

Then reality set in.

"Wait. What am I saying? I can't fall for him again. The first time was a disaster. Just because he waltzes back into town unannounced... just because he's more handsome now than ever, and his voice has deepened to that sexy growl... just because I felt sparks when he touched me and the monitor said he felt it, too... just because he was always *the one*... I can't be considering this! I can't be thinking about getting involved with him again!"

Grace ran a hand through her long hair, verbalizing her dilemma.

"He has demons. His future is unsettled. I can't risk my heart again, but maybe I don't have to. I could be his friend, and I suspect he needs that, more than anything."

Pushing her fingers deep into the tangles, Grace kept thinking aloud.

"I don't even know that I can help him. His scars may be too deep. What if I can't reach him? What if I don't have the energy and the strength to see it through? What if I fail him?"

But there was another thought that kept running through her mind. It snagged in her gut, robbing her breath.

"But what," she wondered aloud, her voice but a whisper, "if I don't even try?"

CHAPTER FOUR

"Good morning, Grace." ER Charge Nurse Laurel Benson greeted her friend as she stepped off the elevators onto the second floor. "Did you get moved into your new place?"

"Slowly but surely," Grace confirmed. "What brings you up this morning?"

"Checking on a patient we saw downstairs yesterday. After a sonogram and echocardiogram, he had a bit of a panic attack. It didn't last long, but I wanted to make sure he was doing all right."

Worry sparked in Grace's eyes. "Oh my gosh! Cruz had a panic attack? Why didn't he tell me? Why wasn't it in his chart?"

Laurel picked up on the intimate tone in Grace's voice. "Cruz, is it?" she teased.

"We… used to know each other. Eons ago."

"Is there a story there?"

Not wanting to elaborate, Grace shook her head. "Not a happy one."

"'Nuff said," Laurel assured her. They walked together toward the nurse's station. "What room is he in?"

"214, but he may not be back from his colonoscopy yet."

Laurel faked a chuckle. "Lucky guy. He's getting the full work-over, huh?"

"I'm not sure he feels *lucky*, but he definitely feels beholden. Apparently, he and Doctor Renaldi served in combat, and Doc saved his life. This is his way of paying him back, in some small measure."

"Doctor Renaldi is doing some big research project, right? The lasting effects of warfare, or something like that?"

"Yes, that's what I understand. A noble endeavor, but can you imagine? Everyone must react differently. I can't begin to imagine the scope of such a project," Grace said, shaking her head in wonder.

"I knew Doctor Renaldi was in the Armed Forces, but I didn't realize he saw action. That makes me admire him even more," Laurel admitted.

"Absolutely." Grace checked the computer behind the desk. "Looks like our patient is all done and back in his room. But I still wonder why the panic attack wasn't on his charts?"

Laurel put a finger to her lips in a 'shh' motion. "I told him I'd keep it on the down-low. Don't rat me out."

"Of course not."

"Good luck on settling into your new place. I'd love to see it, once it's all done."

"Absolutely." Grace smiled at her friend.

As Laurel turned away, Grace wondered about the panic attack. Had something about the tests brought it on? Had all those screens and monitors been a reminder of the warplane Cruz once flew? Was that what brought on the nightmare she had witnessed?

Let this be a reminder to you, Gracie girl. His issues run deep. You'd be wise to remember that.

An hour later, Grace delivered a lunch tray to Cruz's room. She caught him dozing, and he looked so peaceful and so relaxed, she wondered if she had imagined the harsh man from the day before. She knew it was probably the lingering effects of the anesthesia, but even this morning, before the tests, he had seemed mellower.

He was probably too weak by then to put on a stern face, she acknowledged with a smile. She knew prepping for the test was hard on the body.

She placed the tray on the table as quietly as possible and turned to leave.

"Hey." His craggy voice stopped her.

Grace turned back with a smile. "Hey. Sorry to disturb you. I brought lunch."

The crooked smile he offered looked so familiar, so like the boy she had once known, that it did funny things to her heart. "Steak and baked potato?" he asked hopefully, his voice still groggy and muffled.

She couldn't help but laugh. "I think that's a bit ambitious at this point, don't you?"

His hand moved over his flat stomach. "Maybe," he agreed.

"We'll start with something easy, like maybe pudding." She lifted the lid from the plate and reported her findings. "Oh, and rice, as well. Plus, bananas, applesauce, and dry toast."

"No special recipe lime Jell-O?"

There was that lopsided smile again. This time, her heart did a complete somersault.

She should just go. Clearly, he wasn't wide awake yet. Part of her felt guilty, seeing him like this. Trapped in the residual haze of propofol, he might not even know what he said. Part of her felt trapped, thinking nothing good would come from staying. But the biggest part of her, the part mesmerized by that smile and fondly remembering the boy it had once belonged to, felt hopeful.

Against her better judgment, Grace leaned in, taking advantage of the moment. "No," she drawled, her smile hinting at conspiracy, "but I could put in a special request."

His dark eyes studied her for a moment before he spoke, his voice low but surprisingly clear. "You look good, Grace."

His words couldn't have surprised her more. Grace swallowed hard. Yes, she should go now.

"Th—Thank you," she stammered.

"Even more beautiful than ever."

Oh, she should go. But his hand had reached up to touch her, his fingers gently brushing against her face.

He had never touched her face before. There was a sweetness in his gesture that was her undoing. "You look good, too," she replied, breathless.

"Ten years," he murmured. His voice sounded muffled again. "Ten long years."

"Yes."

His eyelids had grown heavy. "I'm sorry, Grace," he mumbled, his hand falling back to his side. "For everything."

Grace stayed for a moment, watching him drift back to sleep. His sleepy apology tore at her heart, ripping open a wound she had thought healed. Obviously, this man still affected her, and that meant he still had the power to hurt her. Every instinct she had told her to turn around and walk away.

But still, she stayed.

Grace was late taking her own lunch. Necrotic wounds had the tendency to dampen her appetite, and the patient in 223 had developed a nasty one, indeed. It was after two o'clock before she pulled out her salad and sat down to eat.

Her phone rang while she was thumbing through Pinterest, looking for ideas on how to decorate her new living room. A fresh start called for fresh decor, but she worked on a shoestring. *That forty dollars over budget didn't grow on trees,* as her father always said. Distracted, she answered the phone with a vague, "Yes?"

"So. You're answering my calls now," a cynical voice greeted her.

Grace regretted not screening the call before accepting it. "Hello, Mother."

"Don't use that tone with me, young lady."

"I'm at work. I'm busy." It was just a tiny white lie, right?

"Shall I call back this evening?"

And devote a full hour to her mother's complaints? Not hardly. "I have a few minutes," Grace relented.

"Did you get moved to your new apartment?"

"Yes, ma'am, I sure did. Dad came over and helped me."

With a slight sniff, Suzanne Stavenaugh ignored the subtle jibe. She had been too busy to offer a hand. "Your father always was as strong as a pack mule. Stubborn as one, too."

"If you called to complain about Dad—"

"I didn't. I called to talk about Hope."

"Of course you did."

Her mother heard the muttered words, even though

Grace uttered them beneath her breath. "Come now, Grace Elizabeth. Jealousy doesn't become you."

"I'm not jealous, Mother. Simply stating facts. What was it you wanted to discuss?"

"We need to coordinate Hope's visit this weekend. I'll pick her up at the airport, of course. Shall I bring her to your house before dinner, or after? Did you want to join us? I have reservations at *Vintage House* at seven."

"I don't get home until seven-thirty." *Thank goodness.*

"And there's no rush to bring her over. She can stop by to see my condo anytime over the weekend."

"She's not coming to *see* your condo, silly. She's *staying* there."

"She's staying with me?" Grace's voice came out in a squeak. "Since when?"

"It's the only solution," her mother said breezily. "I'm having your old bedroom gutted and turned into an office."

"Why don't you use Dad's old office?"

"It's a yoga/gymnastic space now."

"When did all this come about? You didn't mention this when we talked last week. And since when do you do gymnastics?"

"Not me, of course. For Hope. And since we've fired Meredith and I've taken over scheduling all her events, it just makes sense. Hope can practice and work on new routines whenever she's in town."

"Yet she can't stay with you," Grace pointed out.

"Well, I just have the one bedroom. And now you have two, so it makes more sense for her to stay there."

"And yet, every single week, a new hotel pops up in this town. Why can't she get a room in one of them?"

"What kind of hostesses would we be, if we can't even offer her a room in our own homes?" Suzanne sounded truly offended.

"We're not her hostesses, Mother. We're her family. She can sleep on your couch."

"Even if I am her mother, I'm not about to make her sleep on the couch! Your sister is a world-class violinist, and she deserves more than a *couch* when she comes home!"

"Then give her your bed. You sleep on the couch."

"I can't. Your father took it. Which is just as well. I've created a lovely sitting area with armchairs and a small settee. You'll have to come over and see it one day."

Grace pinched her nose, wondering why conversations with her mother always led to a headache. "Look, Mom, I really need to go. And I don't know what to tell you about Hope, but she can't stay at my place. I haven't gotten organized yet, and you know how particular she is."

"You still have three days," her mother pointed out. "She won't be there until Friday evening."

"I'm working all week."

"Maybe I could come over tomorrow evening and help you get things in order." From the tone of her voice, it was obviously a last-resort option.

"Let me get this straight," Grace said, uncharacteristically steamed over her mother's show of favoritism. That, too, she thought was behind her. She'd had twenty-six years to adjust, after all. "You couldn't help me move, but you can help me straighten up for Hope."

"Hope had that concert in Houston. You know I never miss a performance if it's anywhere close by. But I'm home now, and I'd be happy to help you. We don't have to have everything perfect. Just her room, the kitchen, and the living room, in case she wants to entertain friends while she's here."

"Then I suggest we book her a suite at a hotel. And by the way, why isn't the venue putting her up for the weekend? Isn't that customary when she plays a concert?"

"Not when she's here in Aggieland. This is her home!"

Grace shook her head. "A hotel, Mother. Book a hotel."

"But—"

"I don't have a bed in my guest room yet," Grace added, which was true.

"Naturally, you'd want to offer her the master bedroom."

Logic wouldn't work with her mother. Common sense didn't even work. She hated doing it but lying was the only option in a situation like this. "Well, now, that's going to be a problem," Grace said. This wasn't even a little white lie. This was a big, fat, black one. "My mattress was damaged in the move. It has a huge gash, right down the middle. I've been camping out on the floor, in Dad's old Army sleeping bag. You don't know where we could borrow another one, do you?"

"What! No. That would never work!" Her mother was aghast at the very thought. "I'll just have to book a hotel. I'll call the Hilton and see if the penthouse suite is available."

"That's a good idea, Mother," Grace purred. "I'm so glad you came up with a solution. I have to go now. Bye."

Grace took a moment to collect her thoughts and cool down. It never ceased to amaze her, but if possible, her mother was even shallower than her sister was.

Throwing her trash away and pushing her chair back

under the table, she turned to see Cruz standing in the hallway, blocking the doorway to the breakroom. From the look in his dark eyes—part sympathy, part aggravation—she knew he had overheard at least part of her conversation.

"How long have you been standing there?" she asked, her voice slightly defiant.

"Long enough to know you're a very bad liar."

"That's not exactly a bad thing," she said, pushing her way through the door. He stood back, allowing her passage. "It's not like I get a lot of practice. What are you doing roaming the halls?"

"Roaming the halls," he replied. "Doc said I needed to walk. And I'm going stir crazy in that room."

"He's right. Walking is the best thing you can do after a scope. It helps displace the gas."

He fell into step beside her. "So, your mom's trying to pawn your sister off on you, huh?"

"Something like that."

"Too bad about your mattress. You should sue the moving company." If she didn't know better, she could have sworn his eyes glittered with humor. She didn't think the adult Cruz was in the habit of teasing.

"Which consisted of me, my father, and one of my former neighbors. I paid them in pizza."

"Then it's a good thing your mattress wasn't really ripped."

"It sort of was," she denied. Pursing her lips, she decided, "Come to think of it, that could have been a loose thread."

To her surprise, Cruz barked out a shout of laughter. The sound was so unexpected, she almost tripped on her own feet.

"You okay?" he asked.

"Rubber soles," she murmured. "Sometimes they catch on these tile floors."

This time, there was no denying the humor dancing in his dark eyes. "Like I said, you're a terrible liar."

"So, what's next on the agenda? What's Doctor Renaldi pulling from his bag of tricks tomorrow?"

"Tomorrow's the easy day. Physical endurance."

"Easy?" Grace hooted. Quite without knowing it, she walked right past the nurse's station.

"I'm used to testing my physical limits. Give me a treadmill or a rock wall, and I'm good."

"Ah, but I've heard tales. I hear that Deana in Cardiology is a real drill sergeant on the treadmill."

"Sounds right up my alley."

Grace looked over at him with a thoughtful expression. "I guess it would be, wouldn't it?" Without a doubt, he was in excellent physical condition. He wasn't even limping. She had to wonder what had happened yesterday with his thigh, but she wasn't about to ask. They were having a pleasant conversation, reminiscent of old times.

"So, I take it your mom kept the house?" Cruz asked.

"Wow. You must have heard the entire conversation. But in answer to your question, yes. Mom got the house, Dad apparently got the couch, and he now lives in the Edelweiss neighborhood."

Cruz puckered his brow. "Where's that?"

"It really has been a long time since you've been back," Grace chuckled. "You need to get out and explore before you leave town."

"I may do that. Where's your new place?"

"Probably nowhere you ever heard of," she quipped. "In fact, it was probably a hay meadow when you left."

"Huh. I may have hauled hay out of it."

43

"Really? You hauled hay?"

His broad shoulders shrugged in an off-handed manner. "I was never one to work in a fast-food joint or some shoe department. In the summers, I baled and hauled hay, and in the winter, when I could fit it around my school schedule, I worked at a horse stable."

"I guess that's how you had all those muscles, even way back then," she said with a grin. Without thinking, she reached up and touched his thick biceps. She intended to give them a playful pat, but to her chagrin, her fingers lingered in what was almost a stroke.

"Aw, you noticed."

Realizing what she had said and done, Grace jerked her hand back. She didn't even try to decipher the meaning hidden within his dry tone. It could have been snide, could have been flirtatious. She was too busy praying the floor would open and swallow her whole to give it much thought.

They had reached the end of the hallway, opposite from her assigned station. Grace glanced around in confusion, wondering how they had gotten here.

"I'm on my fourth lap," he offered, turning to make a return lap down the parallel hall.

Pride kept her from admitting to a mental lapse in time and space, particularly after all but fondling him. Pretending to need something down the adjacent hallway to their left, she motioned in the general direction of ICU. "I'm going this way."

"By all means," he said, eyes twinkling in a way that said he saw right through her excuse. He stopped with a gallant wave, allowing her to go first.

She couldn't resist a sugary but spiteful reply. "Would you like me to bring you some of that lime Jell-O when you're through with your walk?" she offered.

His eyes narrowed. "Did you come to my room earlier?"

"I brought your lunch tray," she hedged. "But you were sleeping."

He studied her for a moment, clearly not believing she told the full story. He finally nodded, and Grace turned to go, eager to escape his thoughtful gaze.

She hadn't gone far when his voice floated down the hallway behind her. "By the way," he called.

Grace slowed her steps, but she didn't turn around.

"I wasn't really asleep."

She had no idea how to respond, so she kept slowly walking forward.

"And," Cruz added, just loud enough that his voice carried, even when it dropped to a gravelly low, "I meant what I said."

Darn those rubber soles! They really did catch on the tile floors.

CHAPTER FIVE

"I wasn't really asleep."

Cruz repeated the words in disbelief. Why had he said such a thing? He thumped himself upside the head, hoping to knock some sense into it.

"I can't believe I actually admitted that to her," he grumbled aloud. "What is wrong with me? I have no intentions of getting involved with her again, and I refuse to lead her on. I'm a world-class idiot."

"Aw, don't be so hard on yourself."

Cruz whirled around to see his old Army buddy grinning at him.

"Where did you come from? What do you mean sneaking up on me like that?" Cruz growled.

"I work here," Joe Renaldi reminded him. Still grinning, he pointed to the shoes peeking out from beneath his shrubs. "It's the special rubber soles."

"Y'all use that excuse a lot around here, don't you?"

Not understanding, his friend cocked his head. "Huh?"

"Never mind," Cruz grunted.

Joe fell into step beside his friend. "Who's the 'her' in

your one-sided conversation?" he inquired.

"Just a girl I used to know."

"They're never *just a girl*, not if they have you talking to yourself." Joe cocked his head to the side. "That's right," he remembered. "You're originally from Bryan, aren't you?"

Still grumbling, Cruz didn't comment directly. "Why did you have to pick this hospital to work at? Why not San Antonio? Or Galveston? Anywhere, but where she works."

"Oh-ho!" Joe hooted, throwing back his head with laughter. "She works here? She's a nurse here? A tech? Wait. It's not Doctor Sherwood, is it? Because I was thinking about asking her out, but I don't want to step on any toes. Tell me, and I'll back off." He held his arms up in surrender fashion.

"Put your arms down. It's not the doctor."

When Cruz offered nothing more, his friend prompted. "So?"

"So, what?"

"So, who is she?"

Cruz refused to say a word as they passed the nurse's station. Doctor Renaldi craned his neck to see who was on duty, speaking only in response to the nurse's greetings and mentally eliminating the few he saw. He waited until they reached Cruz's room to demand, "Okay, you've kept me in suspense long enough. Who is she?"

"You're persistent, you know that?"

"Hey, we have a psych evaluation coming up. Can't have her messing with your head."

"Too late," Cruz muttered, collapsing onto his bed.

"Now you *have* to tell me!" Joe insisted.

Cruz glared at his friend. "This isn't a joke."

The teasing light faded from Joe's eyes. "I can see that. This girl was really special to you, wasn't she?"

"It was a long time ago."

"Not long enough, apparently. Is she single?"

"She says she is."

"So, you've asked." Joe observed with a sage nod.

Cruz shrugged. "It came up in conversation."

The doctor helped himself to the swivel chair, turning it so he could persist with his line of questioning. "I'll tell you what I know about her, if you'll give me a name," he offered.

Obviously reluctant, Cruz finally gave in. "Grace. Grace Stavenaugh, one of the nurses here."

"Yeah. Yeah, I know Grace."

"But what?" Cruz asked sharply. "Why the stunned look?"

"I just... she doesn't seem your type, is all."

"How would you know what my 'type' is?" Cruz asked, his tone irritable. "I don't have a type."

Realizing he waded deep waters, Joe gave an amicable nod. "Okay. Okay. You're right. And, yes. Grace is an intelligent, beautiful woman and an excellent nurse. Her caring and compassionate nature makes her a favorite with our patients."

Cruz arched a cynical brow. "Oh, so *clearly* not my type, huh? Thanks, buddy."

"That's not what I meant. I just... I just can't see Grace doing you wrong. She doesn't have a mean bone in her body. I can't see her breaking your heart, is all."

"It was a long time ago," Cruz muttered. He stared out the window, his eyes clouded with visions of the past.

"But you still care about her."

A nerve worked in his tightly clenched jaw. It was on

the tip of his tongue to deny the claim, but Joe was one of his closest friends, and Cruz didn't have many. Besides, what good would it do to lie? This week was about evaluation and exploration and, for Cruz, about finding a way to rebuild his life outside the Army. He could start by being honest.

The breath swooshed from his lungs. "It would appear that way."

Cruz missed the tiny smile crossing Joe's face at his stiff admission. He was busy coming to terms with the enormity of his statement. *He still cared about Grace.*

"What do you plan to do about it?" his friend asked.

"There's not much I *can* do about it. I burned that bridge ten years ago. I betrayed her, and I doubt she can ever forgive me."

New understanding dawned in Joe's eyes. "You broke her heart, not the other way around."

"I think both our hearts took a pretty hard lick."

"Look. I can't speak for the past. And you can't change it. But I can tell you that you have the future ahead of you, and that you have the power to change its course. If you want this woman in your future, you may have to shut one door in order to open another."

"It's not that simple."

"Why not?" Joe demanded.

"Her family. She, uh, has this sister…"

Joe dropped his head back with a groan. "Tell me you didn't."

His answer came swiftly. "I didn't. But—"

"You wanted to? Look, you're only hu—"

Cruz interrupted any platitudes his friend might offer in efforts to make him feel better about himself. "No!" Cruz said irritably. "It was never about the sister. Okay. Maybe at first," he amended, "but that changed as soon

as I met Grace. But you don't understand. Her family…"
He stopped, shaking his head with the memory of it all.

Joe knew only bits and pieces of Cruz's past. His
parents had given up hope of ever having a child when
his fifty-year-old mother had finally come up pregnant. It
was a difficult birth from which his mother never
recovered; she passed away while Cruz was a toddler.
His father had done a fine job of raising a child alone,
but money was never in excess. When it came to
spending time with his son or working overtime, Dave
Colton always chose his son.

"I know this," Joe said, his tone confident. "Grace
Stavenaugh is no snob. Even if her sister is famous—yes,
of course I know who she is—I can't see Grace letting
something like social status make a difference to her."

"Of course not. That wasn't it. It may have come to
that, at least with her mother, if our relationship had ever
gotten that far. But that's the thing." Cruz dropped his
head in shame. His voice was raw when he explained, "I
ran out on her, before we ever had the chance to see
where it could go. I abandoned her."

"That sounds a bit dramatic, my friend. Are you sure
you're remembering things the way they really
happened?"

"Because being held prisoner in enemy camp didn't
give me enough time to think," Cruz put in dryly.

"Maybe it gave you too much time to think," his
friend offered quietly. "I'm not saying this is what
happened, but sometimes, especially in horrific
conditions like the ones you endured, our mind will twist
some of the details. Even in the best of circumstances,
memories fade. Viewpoints get skewed. Little things take
on a life of their own and get blown out of proportion.
You remember it as betrayal by running out on her. She

may remember it less harshly."

"I doubt it." Cruz's voice was flat. "You didn't see the look on her face that night." Even now, he closed his eyes, blocking the painful memory from his mind.

The conversation came to a halt as a technician knocked on the door and poked her head inside. "Radiology! We need to get a few more X-rays, Mr. Colton."

Joe unfolded his long body from the chair, slapping his hands against his legs. "That, by the way, was what I was coming to tell you. I need more pictures, my friend."

Cruz simply sighed. Who knew his bones were so photogenic?

After a round of X-rays and a MRI, Cruz settled back into his room and took out his laptop computer. He pulled up his email account and scoured through several promotional offers, a reminder for his upcoming appointment with a financial planner, four offers of employment, and two suggestions from Amazon on what books to read next. Most he sent to the trash folder.

Just for a moment, he let his mind wander back, to a time when he didn't depend on the international giant to make book recommendations for him. He had Grace for that. They spent many hours, discussing potential reading material or sharing opinions on favorite passages and favorite authors.

Why hadn't he ever told her how he felt? Why hadn't he just reached out and held her hand? The few times their hands touched—granted, often by his own design—one or both of them had jerked their hands away immediately, as if burned by the other's touch.

Even now, he could feel the heat that radiated up his arm and warmed a spot in his heart. Why hadn't he just taken a chance? If only he had it to do over again…

"Knock, knock."

He must have conjured her up. Grace's blond head appeared in the doorway. "Am I interrupting something?"

"Just the latest and greatest from Amazon," he said, pressing the delete button.

A mischievous grin lit her face. "Do you ever wonder how we survived without it? What did we do back in the day, when we needed something, and we needed it *now*?"

"I think we went out to the stores and bought it."

"Maybe. But the selection just wasn't the same. There weren't literally one thousand and thirteen of *every* single item we could ever imagine. And no stars to tell us how other people rated them!"

"And they wonder why peer pressure and public opinion has overruled common sense," Cruz remarked dryly.

"Exactly! No one can think for themselves anymore. They have to see what the reviews say, and how many stars something rates." Grace shook her head with exasperation. Then she struck a pose with her finger to her cheek and a twinkle in her eyes. "That reminds me. Don't forget to leave your review on our services here today, sir."

With a chuckle, Cruz said, "Bring me a steak and baked potato, and I promise to give you a five-star rating."

"Is that a bribe?"

"That depends. Is it working?"

When Grace laughed, it brought back so many good memories that his heart ached, trying to collect and store them all.

"I'll see what I can do," she promised. "I just came in to check on you. Since you're not sick, you don't require our normal routine," she pointed out. "I don't want to neglect you, but I also don't want to bug you."

"You're not bugging me."

Her smile spread wide. "Good. So, can I bring you anything? You'll be pleased to know you're no longer restricted to yellow and green Jell-O. I can now offer you the full array of strawberry, black cherry, and orange."

"You make them sound so appealing, but I think I'll pass. I'm about Jell-O'ed out."

Grace pretended to be at a loss. She propped her hands onto slender hips and said, "Gee. People don't usually turn down my offer of *five* different kinds of Jell-O. It's a veritable smorgasbord of gelatin delight. But if you don't want Jell-O, then I guess I'll go."

She made a last-ditch offer of crackers or some other something, but Cruz was no longer listening. He was scrambling for ideas of how to detain her in his room. Her easy laughter and funny personality filled the shadowed corners he hadn't realized were so empty. The same could be said for his heart.

"There is one thing…" he said, quickly clicking on the first e-mail he saw from Amazon. "I don't know if you still read like you used to—"

"I do."

"Okay, good. Amazon sent this as suggested reading. I was wondering if you'd read it and what you thought about it." He angled the computer only slightly, so she had to move in closer to see the screen. Cruz greedily inhaled a deep breath of her unique fragrance, a mix of lemon and sunshine with just a hint of antiseptic. Clean and fresh.

Tiny lines of confusion wrinkled her brow, as she tilted her head a fraction and debated the book's merits. "Well," she concluded, "I don't usually read aircraft manuals, but it has forty-five reviews, and most are four stars or better. That is, of course, if you don't want to think for yourself and just take other people's word for it."

The smile she flashed him was so blindingly beautiful, it took a full moment for her words to register.

"Huh?" He jerked his eyes back to the device, where, as he feared, a manual for a military-type hovercraft filled the screen. "I, uh, must have clicked the wrong message," he mumbled lamely.

"Good. Because I know *nothing* about airplanes," she confessed, her hazel eyes dancing with mischief. They appeared bluer today than yesterday, probably because of the blue scrubs she wore. Or perhaps it was the reflection of his own navy t-shirt. (Joe had at least spared him the indignity of wearing a hospital gown during his stay.) She stood close enough that he could see the little flecks of color in the irises. Could almost count the individual fringe of lashes fanning out from her lids. While he stared up at her in wonder, she continued, "All I know is how to press the call button. That, I've got down." She raised a long finger to demonstrate.

He could think of nothing intelligible to say. Even his mind was scrambled by her nearness.

"Hey," she said, as a thought occurred to her. She lightly slapped the back of her hand against his upper arm, leaving it there as she went on, "Speaking of airplanes. When was the last time you were at Easterwood Airport? Did you fly in, or drive?"

"Drove."

"Then you haven't seen the airport lately?"

"As I recall, there isn't much to see."

"That was then, this is now. You really should go out there. It has exploded in size over the last ten years. With the George H. Bush Library here, and with Texas A&M being what it is, it's quite the busy place now."

"I'll have to check it out," he murmured. He was still acutely aware of her hand on his arm. His eyes drifted that way.

Seeing the direction of his gaze, Grace started to pull her hand away. "Oh! I'm sorry."

Doing what he should have done years ago, Cruz moved quickly. He kept her hand in place by covering it with his own. His dark eyes met hers. "I'm not," he told her.

He saw her draw in an unsteady breath. She looked suddenly nervous—the same way he felt—but she didn't pull away. After a long moment, she relaxed and even offered a smile. "It may not be an exciting airplane manual, but I did read a good book recently. Have you read *The Shack*?"

"No. I've heard about it, but I haven't bought it yet."

"You should. It's really good. I could lend you my e-copy. Which do you prefer? Physical books or e-books?"

"Definitely physical. I like to touch a book. Hold it in my hands." His fingers stroked along the backs of hers as he spoke, the gesture so natural he didn't realize he did it. Touching her felt so *right*.

"So do I, but e-books are so much more practical. I absolutely adore my Kindle reader!" If his touch affected her, she didn't let on. She spent the next several minutes extolling the virtues of electronic readers and the benefits of carrying around hundreds, if not thousands, of books in less space than that of one thin paperback. She remained at his side, hands still touching, as he thought of questions to ask, some of them quite inane. Anything to keep her there.

A tone sounded in the hallway, followed by a page. Grace heard her name called. To her chagrin, they requested her presence back at the nurse's station.

"Oops. Guess I have been in here a while. I need to go."

Cruz reluctantly moved his hand from hers. "Sounds like it. Sorry to monopolize you like that."

"No worries!" she said brightly.

That smile lingered in his thoughts, long after she had gone.

CHAPTER SIX

A flurry of activity late in the day had Grace swamped. She had a demanding new patient on the floor, helped celebrate in an impromptu "release party" for sweet Dierra, transferred the patient with the necrotic wound to surgery, and comforted a frightened young boy waiting for his parents to arrive. By the time she completed her normal end-of-shift duties, it was well past seven when Grace finally clocked out.

She wasn't certain why, but she took the long route to the elevators. The route that took her past Cruz's room.

She was playing with fire. Last night, she convinced herself she could be his friend, nothing more. But that was before she found him all groggy and adorable. He wore that lopsided smile when his guard was down. And he said the sweetest things. Things that made her trip over her own feet and talk for five minutes about the simple thirty-second process of downloading an e-book.

As if neither of those things were pathetic enough, here she was, outside his door.

And here she was, giving in to impulse, popping her head inside.

"Hey," she said.

"Hey." Cruz looked up in surprise, darting his eyes to his watch. "Aren't you here a little late?"

"It feels *way* late," she said.

"You can come in," he invited, closing his laptop.

She went straight to the couch and collapsed. "I may never get up," she warned, already resting her head. "If I had the energy, I would peel myself off here, go home, draw a hot bath, and sleep in the tub."

"I think the couch is definitely safer," was his dry reply. "I hear it pulls out to a bed."

"Hospitals have come a long way, haven't they?" she mused. "I had surgery once when I was a kid. They didn't encourage guests spending the night, but if they did, they had to sleep on a tiny little cot and or in a straight-back chair. My mom stayed one night on the rickety little cot. Says it was the worst night's rest she ever had."

"And after that?"

"I stayed alone." For some ridiculous reason, the admission brought a mist to her eyes. Grace blinked it away in rapid fashion.

He didn't have to tell her how sorry he was. How his heart smarted at the admission, right along with hers. She could hear the caring in his low voice. "That was when you broke your arm, right?"

Her head came up. Her eyes went wide. "How could you possibly know that?"

Cruz shrugged his shoulders, drawing her eye to their wide breadth. "I remember you telling me about it."

"But—But that was a decade ago!" she sputtered.

"You'd be surprised at everything I remember, Grace."

The deep timbre of his voice awakened all her nerve

endings, reviving her weary body like a jolt of lightning. Grace slowly pulled herself upright, cautioning herself to play it cool.

"I, uh, wasn't sure you ...enjoyed..."—she didn't dare use the word 'cherished'—"our conversations as much as I did."

"I did."

It was on the tip of her tongue. She wanted to say it so badly. She wanted to ask him *why*.

Why he had never spoken up. *Why* he had made her wonder, fearing the attraction was all one-sided. *Why* he had chosen Hope that night.

But Grace had learned, long ago, to never ask a question if she weren't prepared to know the answer.

She kept quiet, waiting for Cruz to say something more.

He changed the subject. "How long have you been a nurse?"

She consulted the ceiling, pretending to count in her head. "Does that include the years I spent bandaging teddy bears and Barbie dolls?"

"No. And the time you pulled that splinter from my hand doesn't count, either."

"Oh. Well, in that case... almost six years."

"All at this hospital?"

"No, *Texas General* is only in its second year. But I did start here in town. With any luck, I'll finish my career here, too."

"No dreams of traveling the world?"

"Nope. I've watched Hope traipse from town to town, never settling anyplace long enough to call home. She finds it exciting. I would find it exhausting."

"You and your sister have always been so different," Cruz murmured, his dark eyes studying her.

Grace squirmed beneath his intense gaze. She didn't need to be reminded of her shortcomings. Lifting her chin in a rare show of defiance, Grace made no apology. "I confess to being a homebody at heart. Some people thrive on the heat and sizzle of the spotlight. I prefer the fuzzy softness of the shadows."

"You're right. Hard angles and harsh lights aren't your style." Before she could determine if the words were an insult or a compliment, he continued. The warmth in his voice and the sincerity in his eyes left no doubt. "But when I look at you, I don't see shadows. I see nothing but sunshine."

His praise felt much too good. It brought a flush to her skin as warmth infused her heart. Warning herself about getting too close to the flame, Grace did her best to hide her response. "Well, this little ray of sunshine is all but fading," she proclaimed. "Do you see that? My foot is almost out the door. Now to make the rest of me follow…"

Cruz turned his attention to the doorway, playing along with her charade. He, too, pretended the admission hadn't moved him. "Ah, yes. I think I see it. Another hour or so, and you should be all but gone."

"Let me know when I leave. In the meantime, I think I'll just take a little nap." She rested her head again, giving her racing heart time to adjust.

"I don't think so," Cruz informed her.

Her head popped up to see if he was as serious as he sounded. If not for the tiniest flicker of amusement in his dark gaze, even his facial expression made it difficult to tell. "Doc gave me strict orders to stay awake until ten o'clock, at which time it's lights out. If I can't doze, you can't."

Grace narrowed her eyes in suspicion. "Why do I

suspect you rarely *doze* before bedtime, anyway?"

"You might be surprised. I've learned the value of a random power nap. Sometimes it makes the difference between staying alert during a sensitive mission or being slow to respond. Mistakes like that can cost a pilot his life."

"Did you enjoy being a fighter pilot?"

A long moment passed before Cruz answered. His words were measured. "I loved the strategic maneuvering. I loved flying the aircrafts. I hated the fighting."

"I can understand that." Grace picked at a thread on her pants. "Did you always want to be in the military? A pilot?" Her voice was soft as she mentioned the past. "I don't remember you talking about it much."

He shrugged, unwittingly drawing her attention to his broadened shoulders. "I was always interested in serving my country, but I didn't give it serious thought until an Army recruiter came to campus. I liked what he had to say, and one thing led to another. And after…" He paused as a muscle worked in his jaw. "It just made sense for me to sign up," he concluded.

"How long were you in Iraq?"

"Far too long."

"I would imagine one week would be too long," she commiserated softly.

"You have no idea."

"I'd like to hear about it, if you'd like to tell me."

"I don't." His face was shuttered.

"Fair enough. Just know the offer stands. I'm a pretty good listener, you know."

"I remember."

Grace knew when to change the subject. With a sudden grin, she asked, "Do you remember when I helped you study for your presentation in government class? You had to give a speech, and I was your sounding board."

"As I recall, you ended up rewriting about half of it."

"But you passed with flying colors," she pointed out smugly.

"I did."

The corners of her mouth crinkled even more. "Two years later, I took the same class. I may have borrowed a few points from your speech when crafting my own."

"Did old man Foley recognize it?"

"He kept watching me closely and cocking his head to the side, like he was trying to place where he had heard the words before, but he never called me on it. I, too, passed with ease."

"So, it was a win-win situation for both of us."

"Absolutely."

"I always knew we were a good pair."

The moment the words were out, the air grew still. Grace studied the thread again, and Cruz scowled as he readjusted his legs. The past stood between them like a giant elephant, and neither knew how to go around it. For now, it seemed easiest to simply ignore it.

Grace recovered first, managing to paste on a bright smile. "Did you order that aircraft manual you had your eye on?"

"No, but I did look at electronic readers. I'm thinking of ordering a Kindle. Now to decide which model to buy."

"You know me. I prefer the plain, simple, no-frill readers."

Cruz cocked his dark head to one side as he demanded, "Why do you always do that?"

"Do what?"

"Downplay your strengths. Paint yourself as the plain, dowdy, ugly duckling."

Clearly uncomfortable with his observation, Grace squirmed in her seat. "I don't know what you're talking about."

"Yes, you do. You've always done it. To hear you tell it, you all but blend into the shadows, when nothing could be further from the truth. Why do you do that?"

Sadly lacking the quality for which she was named, Grace snorted. "You saw the house I grew up in. I *was* the ugly duckling in the shadows."

"That was before I ever met you, then."

Grace pushed to her feet, fueled by his ridiculous claim. "How can you say that? Hope was the pretty one. I was the smart one. That's just the way it was."

"Being pretty and being smart are not mutually exclusive," Cruz pointed out. "You're the perfect example of a beautiful, intelligent woman. Clearly both."

Her tone was sardonic. "Is this the *Ugly Duckling Grows Up to be a Beautiful Swan* inspirational speech they always give the homely girls in junior high?"

"Hardly appropriate in this case. For as long as I've known you, you've always been a beautiful swan."

Grace gave another snort. "They let you fly with those bad eyes of yours?"

"Okay, so now I think you're just fishing for compliments," Cruz accused. "Not flowery enough for you? Do you prefer gorgeous? Ravishing?"

"I am *not* fishing for compliments! And this conversation has gotten completely out of hand." For emphasis, Grace stomped her foot. The rubber sole made it less effective than she hoped, but she wasn't giving up. She crossed her arms with a sniff. "As I recall, we were talking about e-readers."

"You like a plain, no-frill reader. A nice contrast to what you see in the mirror every day."

So, the adult Cruz *did* occasionally tease. To her surprise, his eyes glittered with humor, daring her to argue with him.

"Completely out of hand," she muttered, rolling her eyes. "And with that, I think it's time for me to go."

"Don't rush out just because I offer you a compliment."

"I'm not. I'm rushing out because you're stubborn and because I'm exhausted."

And because I am entirely too flattered by your compliments.

"I never thought you were one to run from a challenge." Once started, Cruz seemed to enjoy teasing her.

"I can assure you. I am much too tired to *run* from anything. That's why I'm going home and going to bed."

"And effectively ending this conversation," he pointed out.

"One could hope."

As she reached the door, Cruz called out a piece of advice. "If you sleep in your bathtub, at least drain the water first."

CHAPTER SEVEN

"Mmm-mmm. Now *that's* what I like to see so early in the morning!" Shanae chuckled as she stepped behind the desk and discreetly nodded toward the man walking the hall.

Cruz clipped along at a brisk pace, exposing only a portion of the wires he wore as he participated in the warm-up portion of the tests. The rest of the gadgets and monitors were hidden beneath a close-fitting gray tee, already dampened with sweat and clinging to his muscled abs. Shorts and athletic shoes revealed long, tanned legs that were sinewy and heavily muscled. The mid-thigh shorts offered a clear view of an unmistakable, ugly scar that started on the outer side just above the knee, slashed across the front of his leg, and disappeared beneath the hem. That single mar to perfection, horrific though it was, did little to deter the multiple eyes ogling him amid wistful sighs.

"We've had a sudden interest in working on charts this morning," Cami noted wryly, referencing the crowded space within the nurse's station. Opening to both hallways, it offered an optimal view of the man circling the wing. Women lined up along the desk, pretending to look at monitors and computer screens as their eyes covertly followed his every step.

"After round two, even little Mrs. Yamani pushed her walker to the doorway and camped out for the long haul," Grace pointed out. And who could blame her? It took everything she had not to ogle Cruz herself, but she felt she owed him that much respect. No need joining her co-workers in eyeballing him as if he were a Versace original.

"Why are you the only one not fanning herself and trying to put her eyeballs back in her head?" Shanae demanded, propping a fist onto her generous hip. "You blind, girl? Even Martha over there is getting an eyeful, and she's been happily married for half a century!"

"I'm not blind."

"And yet you sit there like a bump on the log. Did you not take my advice the other day?" After a couple of days off, Shanae seemed insulted that her suggestion went unheeded. "Girl, you may not be in the market for a new man, but it sure don't hurt to window shop. 'Specially when the merchandise looks like *that*." She hitched a thumb over her shoulder and made an expressive statement with a simple pose.

"Oh, he's not a *new* man," Cami pitched in, her eyes taking on a teasing light. She rolled her chair closer and stage-whispered, "Grace knew him back in the day. They go *way* back." She crossed her fingers to show how close they had once been.

"Oooh, girl! Do tell!" Shanae cackled in delight.

"There's nothing to tell." Grace's reply was uncharacteristically sharp.

Shanae wasn't fooled. "Oh, that tone says there is definitely something to tell." When she saw the daggers shooting from Grace's hazel eyes, however, she wisely backed off. "Okay. Okay. Calm down. I won't pry. When you're ready, you can give us the whole sordid story."

Undaunted, Cami just grinned. "Until then, you can go back to your charts and we'll go back to our view."

She pushed her chair away as Grace replied primly, "I'd prefer we all go back to our work. We have patients, after all."

"Not many. It's actually a rather quiet day."

"Then go right ahead." Grace made a welcome gesture with her arm, her voice heavy with sarcasm. "I'm sure Cruz doesn't mind one bit, being drooled over like he's prime rib."

"Oh, girl," Shanae corrected, watching as Cruz disappeared down the hall. "That man is definitely filet mignon."

Grace ignored her friends' antics. She knew it was irrational, but she was jealous of their interest in Cruz. He certainly wasn't the first patient to cause a stir among the staff—there was a local police detective who did the same—but this felt personal. She had known Cruz first, and she knew him best, even if it had been the younger version of Cruz Colton. Several times yesterday, she caught a glimpse of her old friend, but the man was so much different from the boy she had once known. That difference was at once scary and exciting, and she felt oddly territorial of those changes.

After a couple more rounds, a physical therapist came and whisked Cruz away. There was a collective sigh heard throughout the wing when the elevator doors closed. Old Mrs. Yamani shuffled back to her bed, several doors closed along the hallway, and the nurses left their station in a sudden flurry of activity.

Without Cruz there to stir imaginations and tease senses, Grace breathed a sigh of relief.

By the time Cruz returned that afternoon, he was obviously tired. He tried hiding it, but Grace noticed the drawn look around his mouth and the slight limp in his step. She allowed him time to get settled and to catch his breath before she pushed a large monitoring device into his room.

"I see you survived," she said with a smile, keeping her voice light.

His was a grunt. "Barely."

She reached into her scrubs' pocket. "I brought juice. Doctor's orders, by the way."

"What I really want is water."

"I have that, too." Her smile brightened as she produced a fresh tumbler of iced water. "I need to take your vitals and hook you up to this monitor."

"Another one?" he asked in irritation.

"Take it up with your buddy." She defended her actions as she assembled the necessary items at his bedside. "Can you raise your shirt, please?"

With a bit of a growl, Cruz sat up and removed the entire offending garment. "Happy?" he all but snarled.

"It does make it easier." She studied the broad chest to select the best spot to place the foam electrodes, trying hard not to notice its impressive muscle tone. A thick patch of dark curls stretched across his chest's surface, interrupted in odd patches to accommodate previous modules.

"How sensitive are you to the adhesives?" she asked. "I can either pick on an old place, possibly making the irritation worse, or I can clear a new patch. Which shall it be?"

"I'm tough," he insisted. "I can handle a little thing like glue."

Despite the rough edge in his voice, she heard the fatigue behind it. Tough or not, the difficult regimen had taken its toll on his body.

Grace willed her hands not to tremble when she touched him. She leaned over him to cleanse the spot with an alcohol wipe, position the stickers, and attach the needed wires. Having difficulty snapping the leads in place, she moved even closer, brushing against his bared waist. Grace cleared her throat, pretending not to swallow a gasp of awareness. Both pretended not to notice the quickened heart rate displayed on his monitor.

"Finally!" she cried in triumph, feeling the snap beneath her fingertips.

"You have condensation on your shirt," he murmured, touching the droplets left by the water pitcher. He applied no force, but the magnetic pull of his touch held Grace in place.

"I, uh, didn't mean to get you wet," she apologized lamely.

"You didn't."

Because the steam evaporated it! She wanted to shout the acknowledgment, but of course, she said nothing. Cruz was acutely aware of the sizzle between them, same as she.

"I'll leave this on for about thirty minutes, or until you've completely relaxed. The purpose is to record you at rest and fully at ease."

"Then you'd better leave."

The rude comment took her by surprise. Grace batted her eyes a time or two, blinking away the unbidden and ridiculous sting of tears. "Oh. Yes. Of course."

Realizing how the words sounded, Cruz closed his eyes and allowed his hand to fall. In truth, he meant that her nearness always energized him, putting his senses on high alert. But to explain that would complicate things between them even further. He felt trapped in that wedge of a rock and hard place again.

"Grace..."

"No, you're right. You need time to unwind after that strenuous workout. You were at it for hours." She spoke quickly, collecting her trash without daring to look him in the face. "I'll dim the lights and let you rest." Before he could protest, she was at the door. "Be back in an hour."

Grace shut the door as she left, mentally berating herself for letting his gruff remark hurt so much. She knew he must be exhausted. She knew his pride must have been smarting, right along with his thigh. She knew he wasn't interested in a relationship with her. Not now, and obviously not then, either.

These sparks flying around between them were nothing but leftover embers from bridges burned, a decade past.

She knew she took the coward's way out, but when she returned, she took a respiratory therapist with her. Grace unhooked the monitor, recorded Cruz's vitals, and left the therapist there with him to discuss breathing techniques.

She didn't return until she delivered his evening meal. By then, she had come to terms with his gruff dismissal and had renewed her decision to simply be his friend. He was a returning soldier of war. After a career of sacrifices, he once again volunteered his time and his body, this time in the name of science. If nothing else, she owed him her gratitude and respect.

Friendship, after all, was a two-way street. Whether he returned the gesture was dependent on him, and not something she could force.

On days like this, he made it difficult.

"This is all I get?" Cruz glowered down at the salad she sat before him. "I busted my butt for this test, and this is all Doc can offer me?"

"There's an energy shake to go with it," Grace offered in a timid voice.

"Whatever." In no better mood now than he had been earlier and clearly irritated with his meager meal, Cruz ripped the paper from around his eating utensils. He stabbed the fork into the salad with an angry jab. "Just wait till I see him," he muttered darkly. "If I have the energy, I'm giving Joe a piece of my mind!"

"And with that, I think I'll go…" Grace made a show of tiptoeing from the room, but she thought he was too aggravated to notice. She could still hear him grumbling when she reached the door.

She returned just before she got off shift, this time with a smile and a special surprise.

Cruz sat in the recliner, reading his book. "Another rabbit feast?" he asked, eying the tray in her hands.

"Oh, no," she assured him. "This is something much better."

The tantalizing scent drew his attention. Cruz's expression transformed from a petulant sulk to that of a hinted smile. "Dare I hope? Is that the steak and baked potato you've been promising me?" he asked cautiously.

Grace lifted the domed lid with a flourish. "Ta-da!"

Cruz closed his eyes and took in a deep, flavorful breath. "Okay. I'll give you your stars back."

Grace snapped the lid back down. "You took away my stars?"

"You brought me that wimpy salad. Of course, it cost you your approval rating." He put his hand over hers and lifted the lid again. "But if this tastes half as good as it smells, this is worth all five, and more."

Grace laughed. "I couldn't just let you starve. You had your dinner salad about an hour and a half before the rest of your meal, but that should leave you plenty of room to enjoy your steak. I had it catered from the best steakhouse in town."

"*Sarge's?*" he asked hopefully.

Grace frowned. "No, that burned down about eight years ago and the owners decided not to re-build. But believe me, this is just as good."

"Wait. *You* had this catered?"

"I had it cleared with your doctor," she quickly assured him. "He agreed that it was the least we could do, after all you're going through this week, and all in the name of science."

Cruz took another deep breath. "And believe me. I will enjoy every bite."

"Knock-knock."

The doctor himself appeared in the doorway, carrying a second tray with a covered dome and a tall stool that could double as a table.

Grace smiled in approval. "It looks like you'll have a dinner guest this evening. I might even be able to find some sort of dessert for you two gentlemen."

"All taken care of." This came from Cami as she followed behind the doctor, a small cake in her hands.

When Shanae joined them, wearing a huge smile and a twinkle in her eyes, Grace grew suspicious. The second nurse had wine glasses in her hand.

"Yes, indeed," Joe Renaldi agreed, placing his tray upon the stool and standing back with a grin. "You will, indeed, have a dinner guest this evening. What's a proper steak dinner without wine and a beautiful companion?" He pulled a bottle from his deep pockets and uncorked it.

"Your modesty knows no bounds," Cruz said in a dry voice. "I wouldn't quite call you beautiful, bud."

"You wound me." Joe continued to work the cork free, as Shanae deposited the wine glasses and Cami set the cake on the bed tray. She added two small plates and a cake knife.

"However," Joe went on to say, having freed the cork from the bottle and now pouring the wine with a flourish, "even though there are those who would differ, I do not refer to myself." Shanae giggled at his antics, earning herself a bright smile from the good-looking doctor before he continued, "Since Grace thoughtfully suggested we treat you tonight, we thought it was only appropriate to return the gesture. Grace, consider yourself off duty and officially invited for dinner. Sit, sit."

She blinked at him in surprise. "But…"

"Doctor's orders," he barked in mock gruffness. "You both deserve it. Enjoy."

Grace stole a glance at Cruz. She couldn't tell if he was aggravated or pleased, but he pursed his lips and studied his friend with a solemn expression. After a moment, he nodded and dropped the other man's gaze, but not before Grace noticed the brief blink. Wishful thinking, perhaps, but she thought it was a silent expression of thanks between the two friends.

"You two have fun," Shanae said in a singsong voice, waving her fingers as she floated out the door on a giggle. Cami winked at Grace, making her blush, and followed the other woman out the door.

"I didn't think to order a steak for myself," Joe fibbed. "I think I'll drop by and treat myself to dinner. You two enjoy yours before they get cold."

"Thank you," Grace said, truly touched by the doctor's gesture.

"No problem." He grinned. "See you both tomorrow."

After their benefactors were gone and the door shut behind them, Grace remained standing beside the makeshift table.

"Aren't you going to sit down?" Cruz asked.

"I don't have to," she offered. "That was incredibly sweet of them to do this, but if you prefer I leave…"

"Sit."

It wasn't the most gracious of invitations, but she imagined it was the best she would get. Without further ado, she took her place on the small couch. "Looks good," she said, if for no reason but to fill the awkward silence between them.

"It does."

Grace dipped her head in silent thanks, surprised when she looked up and saw Cruz doing the same. His dark head remained bent a few seconds longer than hers did. Something in her softened. Given his profession and the horrors he had seen, she imagined Cruz appreciated life and all its goodness in ways she couldn't begin to comprehend.

Cruz reached for his fork and steak knife without meeting her eyes. "Let's see if this tastes as good as it looks and smells." Grace waited for his reaction, pleased when she saw the look of bliss upon his chiseled face. "Perfection," he announced.

"I'm glad you like it."

He finally met her eyes. "Thank you, Grace," he said

quietly.

"My pleasure."

They shared a look, and Grace thought she saw a smile lifting the corner of his mouth. She lifted her wineglass in salute.

"To all military heroes."

He tipped his glass to hers. "To nurses and health care professionals everywhere."

The sense of a truce settled between them and set the tone for their meal. Cruz asked about other landmarks and businesses in town, places and people he remembered from the past. Some remained, some were but a memory. Grace told him about some of the many changes and the tremendous growth that had taken place in their community as they ate their meal.

"You really should get out and see it," she encouraged him, yet again, as she pushed away her plate. "When are you going back?"

"To where?"

"Uhm, I don't know. Wherever it is you came here from."

A shadow crossed his face, and she wondered if she had said the wrong thing. After refilling his wine glass, Cruz eventually answered, "I came here from the Army. As I am no longer enlisted, I can't exactly go back."

"So, your future is wide open." Her words were soft, but upbeat.

"That's one way of looking at it."

When he offered her more wine, she declined. "How else would you look at it?"

"One could argue that the past is closed."

"One could point out that when one door closes, another opens."

"Or one could just continue to wander, walking

aimlessly down the long corridor of life."

Grace didn't like the shift of their conversation. It had taken a definite downhill turn. "Cake," she murmured. "I think this conversation could use a little cake to sweeten it up."

Before she could hop up and get it, Cruz was up and reaching for the small creation. It boasted chocolate ganache frosting with curls of dark chocolate and fresh strawberries as garnish.

He turned and brought it to the small makeshift table, clearing away her finished tray. After adding plates and the cake knife, he took his seat.

Right there beside her on the couch.

And suddenly much too close for comfort.

CHAPTER EIGHT

With precise care, Grace slid the knife through the three layers of chocolate cake separated by whipped cream and fresh strawberries. "This looks divine," she said, hating it when her voice came out breathless and small.

"You should be a surgeon," Cruz complimented her, examining the perfection of the cut.

Or was he mocking her, knowing fully well how nervous his nearness made her? It was difficult to tell with his dark, unreadable eyes.

"Try it," she encouraged, shoving the plate toward him. "This place makes wonderful cakes. They specialize in this particular one."

"Everyone needs a specialty," he said, voice cryptic as he took the plate from her ever-so-trembling hand.

"And what was yours? In the Army, I mean?" She dared to bring up the subject again, but she was curious about his life and his career, and she was nervous with him sitting so close, their knees all but touching.

"For the past few years, I've taught search and rescue to first responder teams, military and civilian."

Grace was duly impressed. "Really? You do know one of the premier search and rescue teams in the nation is located right here in College Station, right?"

"Of course. I trained most of their instructors. In fact, several of the team members, too."

"You're kidding!" Grace turned toward him, his nearness making her voice more animated than usual. "You should see if they're hiring. Just think. You could move back home."

Home. It was such a strange concept after all these years.

"As a matter of fact, they've already reached out to me," Cruz admitted.

"Really? That's awesome! You're considering taking the job, right?"

He looked uncomfortable. "I'm not sure."

"But why not? Wouldn't you like to come back to the BCS area?"

"I, uh, wasn't sure I'd be welcomed," he said lowly.

She swallowed hard. "Oh."

"Grace."

"You—You don't have to…" Her voice trailed off, uncertain of how to finish. Should she just come out and say it? *You don't have to be sorry for breaking my heart. It never quite healed, but I patched it best I could.*

His gravelly voice was still low. "I owe you an explanation. I should have never just walked out like that."

"I never saw you again after that night." She hadn't intended to say it, but the heartbreak leaked out.

"I joined the Army the next day. I didn't even attend my own high school graduation. They mailed my diploma to me at Boot Camp."

"But… why?" They both knew she was asking about

more than just the missed graduation ceremony.

"I was confused, Grace. I was young and idealistic. But mostly, I was a fool."

Her hazel eyes were troubled. "I don't understand."

"I know you don't." Cruz pushed his hand through his short military-style haircut.

Grace saw the pain in his face. The evening had been so pleasant until now. She hated to ruin it with a speech she wasn't sure she wanted to hear.

"Look," she offered, shaking her head. "It doesn't matter anymore."

"How can you say that?"

"That was a long time ago, Cruz. We grew up, and we moved on. Maybe some things are best left in the past."

"You believe that?"

"What does it matter? I thought… I wanted to believe…" She stopped and started again, before she finally had the courage to continue in a soft, sad voice, "I obviously misinterpreted our friendship. I was foolish to think it could ever be anything more. I should have known you were just another one of my sister's hand—"

Before she could finish her sentence, Cruz leaned in and kissed her. It was soft and sweet, and too short to satisfy either of them. It was the moment she had dreamed about, ten years ago.

It was the moment that left her breathless, even now.

Cruz pulled away, leaning his forehead against hers. "I've wanted to do that for so long now," he confessed. His guttural whisper sent shivers through her.

She didn't know if he meant since they were teenagers, or if he meant since they became reacquainted three days ago. Perhaps he meant just this evening. Perhaps it was his way of thanking her for providing the coveted steak. She wouldn't ruin the moment by asking.

"Me, too," she confessed.

"There's some things you don't—"

"Not tonight," Grace begged, pressing her fingers against his lips. "We've had a nice evening so far. Let's just enjoy it while it lasts."

Cruz clasped her hands in his and kissed her fingers. Their foreheads still touched, so he kept his voice low. "I'm getting released tomorrow afternoon."

"Oh."

Funny, how her heart already missed him, even though he hadn't yet gone.

"I come back in two weeks for another round. I'd like to see you when I do."

"There's a good chance I'll be your nurse again."

"I mean… outside the hospital."

"I'd like that."

Their lips touched for another chaste kiss. "Maybe you could show me around town?"

"Or maybe go apartment hunting?" she suggested. He felt her smile against his lips.

"I don't know about that…" he said, pulling away.

"Tell me you'll at least think about it."

"I'll think about it," he dutifully replied.

"You know," Grace ventured to say, gathering the courage she had lacked a decade ago, "we don't have to wait. I could show you around this weekend, once you get out of here. Do you have to hurry off?"

"Not particularly," he admitted.

"I have the weekend off."

"I thought your sister was coming."

Grace's smile was impish. "All the more reason to have other plans."

Cruz, however, frowned. "I don't want to take you away from your family."

Yet they had no qualms about taking you away from me. The silent reminder was between them, even though neither spoke a word.

"You've met my mother and sister," Grace finally said, her voice low. "Please, take me away." The words weren't spoken in jest.

"I'll ask Joe if I can bunk with him tomorrow night. You get off at seven?"

"Yes." She felt the smile building in her heart, bursting to get out. It made her voice come out hushed and reverent.

"I'll need your address. Can you be ready by eight?"

"Fifteen," she pushed. She would need time to shower and change. She ran her limited wardrobe selections through her head, mentally discarding them, piece by piece. What would she wear?

"Have a particular restaurant in mind? It sounds as if half the places I remember aren't here anymore." His tone was wistful.

"As a matter of fact, I have somewhere in mind. I'll call and see if I can get a reservation."

"Then it's a date?" Cruz's dark gaze was hopeful. Delicious shivers skated across her skin at the deep timbre of his voice.

She had waited for those words for over a decade. Afraid she might blow them away with the slightest breath, Grace nodded and whispered a simple reply, "Yes."

Cruz leaned in again to brush his lips across hers. "I'll look forward to it."

"I should go." Her tone was reluctant.

"I have my psych evaluation tomorrow," Cruz told her. A smile played at the corners of his mouth. "I have a feeling it will go better than expected."

Her reply was a widening smile. She kissed her fingertip and pressed it against his lips. "Good night, Cruz."

She stood, and he started to follow suit. She motioned for him to stay, mindful of his leg. "You've had a rough day. I know my way out."

When he didn't argue, she realized how exhausted he truly was.

"Drive safely going home."

"I will."

"Good night, Grace. Sweet dreams."

When she reached the door, she turned and told him with a bold and playful smile. "They will be now."

Her phone vibrated as she unlocked the front door. With the device still on silent, she couldn't hear the distinctive ringtone Hope insisted everyone use with her contact information. It was a downloaded clip of her best violin concerto. Wiggling the key in the lock, Grace spoke into the phone wedged between her head and shoulder, unaware of the caller on the other end. "Hello?"

Foregoing a proper greeting, her sister launched into the reason for her call. "Do you still have that blue cashmere sweater I loaned you?"

Regretting not screening the call first, Grace sighed. "You mean the 'gently worn' one you gave me for my birthday?"

Hope sniffed in regal dismissal. "You must be confused. I merely loaned it to you."

"Yeah, ribbons and wrapping paper tend to do that with me," Grace drawled. As usual, the sarcasm went over her sister's head. Perhaps because Hope rarely listened when other people spoke.

"I want to wear it while I'm in town." It wasn't a request. Grace classified it more as a summons.

And, suddenly, Grace had endured one summons too many from her demanding older sister. She had a flash of inspiration on what to wear on her date with Cruz.

"Then I'll try not to spill red wine on it tomorrow night," Grace said glibly. "Or barbecue sauce. With any luck, you can spritz it with perfume and borrow it on Saturday."

Hope wasn't amused. "One," she continued in a bored tone, as if pointing out the obvious to a sullen child, "I can't borrow what I already own. Two, I doubt there's a decent dry cleaner in this town to handle such delicate fabric in so short a time. That is a very expensive sweater. Just bring it when we meet for dinner tomorrow night."

"I won't be joining you and Mother for dinner."

"She said you would be late. That's fine. We'll still be having appetizers and drinks when you arrive."

"I won't be arriving, Hope. I have a date."

"You have a date?" The surprise in her voice was too genuine to be intentional, proof that her sister could be condescending and rude without even trying.

"Yes, Hope, I have a date. And I'll be wearing the sweater you gave me, so you'll just have to come up with something else to wear."

"Of course." She agreed so quickly, Grace knew there was an insult soon to come. Hope didn't disappoint. "You need that sweater *far* more than I do. I'll just pull something else from my closet, but I know you don't have that luxury. Now, listen. Don't pair that sweater with jeans, not unless they're dark denim with skinny legs. A nice pair of slacks would be better, but whatever you do, make certain you wear heels. Promise me."

Rolling her eyes, Grace dutifully replied, "I promise."

"Good. And since when did you start dating again? I thought you had sworn off men after that last fiasco."

"I never said that."

"No, but I just assumed…" Hope let the thinly veiled insult trail away.

Grace changed the subject with an abrupt, "Will you see Dad while you're in town?"

"If time allows."

There was a gentleness to Grace's reprimand. "He's still your father, Hope."

"Perhaps you should remind *him* of that," her sister sniffed. "He's made little or no effort to reach out to me, either."

Knowing her sister, that most likely meant their father hadn't shown up on her doorstep with arms full of roses and trinkets, begging for her forgiveness. A simple phone call wouldn't suffice in Hope's eyes.

It wasn't how she wanted to spend her day—not with her sister, anyway—but Grace felt she should at least make the effort. "Maybe you and I could have lunch with him on Sunday."

"I'd have to check my schedule and see if I'm free."

Grace knew that was Hope's way of avoiding any unwanted interaction. She often claimed a 'crazy schedule' when it came to family gatherings and efforts to bond with her or their father. Over the years, Grace had quit trying. Like friendship, belonging to a family was a two-way street. *Blood alone does not a family make*, she reminded herself.

"You're coming to the concert, right?" Hope wanted to know. "I think there are still one or two tickets available."

"They didn't offer you any guest seats?" Grace asked in surprise. "That's strange. I thought they always did."

"Oh, they did. But Claire wants to bring her fiancé and his parents. They're treating me to dinner afterward. I promised the other two tickets to Lyndsey and Craig."

"So, it will be the three of you together again." Grace referred to Hope's two best friends from high school. Though outwardly popular, the threesome was often known as 'mean girls.'

"I knew you would prefer to buy a ticket and show your support for your only sister." Judging from Hope's guileless tone, she was completely sincere.

More like too self-absorbed to think otherwise, Grace acknowledged with another roll of her eyes. Biting back a rebellious smile, she returned her sister's words to her. "Like you, I'd really have to check my schedule."

There was a pouting silence on the other end of the line. "What's up with you?" Hope ultimately asked. "You seem different."

Because I'm finally standing up for myself and not letting you use me for a doormat?

Grace kept the thought to herself. Aloud, she said, "It's been a very busy week at work, and I'm tired. I'm sure they'll invite you back very soon. If I don't make tomorrow night's concert, I'll definitely make the next one."

"Yes, I'm sure I'll be invited back next semester," Hope replied confidently.

"If you decide you're free Sunday afternoon, let me know, and I'll set something up with Dad."

"I doubt I will be, but I'll check."

Grace pretended to believe the empty promise. "Be careful coming in tomorrow."

"If your date cancels, you can always join Mom and

me at *Vintage House*," Hope offered.

Nostrils flared, Grace smiled through clenched teeth. "Thanks, but I doubt that happens."

"You never know. You don't seem to have the best of luck with men."

"Good night, Hope."

"You don't have to get huf—"

She didn't hear the rest of the sister's words. Grace had already hit the *End* button.

CHAPTER NINE

When Grace clocked in the next morning, her director was there to greet her.

"I need a huge favor, Grace," the older woman said.

"Of course. What can I do for you?"

"I need you to work ICU today. Meredith called in sick, and they have a full house. I hate to lose you on the floor, but they need you there."

"Sure. No problem." Grace smiled, but inwardly, she rued the fact she wouldn't see Cruz today.

There's still tonight, she reminded herself. *It's been ten or more years in the making, but I finally have a date with Cruz. What's a few more hours?*

The busy day in ICU flew by, and soon it was time to clock out. Grace hurried home to shower and change clothes.

She slid into the silky cashmere sweater, pairing it with a pair of black jeans. The pants even had skinny legs, just as Hope insisted. Though reluctant to admit it, she knew her sister had great fashion sense. Without second-guessing the advice, Grace found a pair of high-heel boots that once belonged to Hope, completing her ensemble. Silver hoops and a long dangling necklace added the final touch.

Butterflies took flight in her stomach when the doorbell rang. Grace paused a moment before opening the door, practicing a few deep-breathing exercises. She ran an unsteady hand over her hair to smooth down any stray golden strands, gulped in a lungful of air, and opened the door.

Her breath escaped in a single swoosh.

Cruz stood on her doorstep, looking taller and more commanding than she remembered. He wore pressed jeans and a starched white shirt, covered with a brown leather bomber jacket. On some vague level, it occurred to Grace that the jacket was the real thing, but her mind was stuck on the sheer beauty of the man. Tall, dark, and handsome, he was her every dream, come back to life. In a single moment, the last ten years melted away, and she felt like the same teenage girl she was then, completely infatuated with the man on her doorstep.

Grace was too awe-struck to notice how Cruz seemed to experience a similar reaction. His greeting, murmured in a deep, rusty voice, was like a caress. "You look beautiful."

Her reply was little more than a whisper. "So do you."

After a moment of simply staring at one another, Cruz asked, "May I come in?"

Snapping out of her reverie, Grace blushed and stepped aside, motioning him into the apartment. "Of course. Please, come in."

She inhaled the essence of him as he brushed close and filled the small foyer with his overpowering presence.

"Nice place you have," he commented.

Untying her tongue, Grace offered, "Would you like

the grand tour?"

"Sure. If we have time."

"It won't take that long," she assured him, relaxing enough to offer an impish smile. As she led him through the modest space, she apologized, "I haven't had time to decorate yet."

"Looks great, just the way it is."

"But there's hardly a thing on the walls!" She turned in time to see that his eyes were on her, not the sparse decor.

"I didn't notice," he murmured, tying her tongue up in knots again. Right along with her heartstrings.

"We, uh, had better go," she said.

Grace grabbed her purse from the couch, and a light jacket she had draped there. Cruz was quick to help her into it, his hands lingering on her shoulders as he pulled the fabric close around her. Discovering her hair trapped beneath the collar, he carefully pulled the silky locks free, taking a moment to enjoy the faint scent of lemons and sunshine filling his nostrils.

"Where are you taking me, Grace?" The low timbre of his words made them sound more sensual than they should have.

"Uhm, University... Town Center." The answer came out amid halting breaths.

"You'll have to show me the way."

Why did his words sound like they had a hidden meaning? And did his hands truly tremble just now, as he all but fondled her hair, allowing his fingers to twist amid the tresses?

"I will." Her eyes were huge and solemn, begging him to trust her.

They both knew they were talking about more than simple navigational directions.

Herding her to his truck, Cruz held the door as she climbed into the one-ton pickup. They laughed about the convenience of her having legs long enough to boost herself aboard with ease and then they were off, Cruz following her directions to the upscale dining district.

"What is this place? Are we still in College Station?" he teased.

"Most people don't realize this," Grace confided, "but the lighted fountain and reflective pool serves a bigger purpose than just ambiance."

"It's a wishing fountain?" he guessed.

She pursed her lips in thought. "That, too," she admitted. "But actually, that fancy fountain doubles as a storm water detention facility."

"Leave it to Aggie engineers to give it a purposeful function," Cruz smirked, finding a place to park his oversized truck. "I see a half dozen or more restaurants here. Which one are we going to?"

"I thought you might enjoy the hibachi grill. It's really good," she assured him.

Cruz came around to open her door and help her down. "Where you lead," he murmured, "I will follow." For the briefest of moments, he nuzzled his face into the cloud of her hair.

The butterflies took flight again. Grace tamped them down as Cruz took her elbow and ushered her across the parking lot. As they stepped into the plaza area and joined the others milling about the space, his hand moved to the small of her back, sending a thrill through her. They were like any other couple, out for a dinner date on a Friday night.

Requesting a seat at the grill, they had a brief wait before space became available. They made small talk while they waited, discussing preferred restaurants and favorite dishes. Soon, they were shown to their places around the hibachi grill with two other couples, a family of four, and a friendly, engaging chef.

Grace gradually relaxed, enjoying the show as the chef entertained the small crowd with his talents. He sliced and diced with ease, wielding his steel spatula and knife with amazing skill. The outrageous tricks drew exclamations of awe from his audience, particularly the two youngsters at the table. Even Cruz was relaxed, laughing as the chef's hands flew over the food, and the flames, faster than their eyes could track.

At one point, Grace leaned forward in anticipation, amazed at how the chef could stack the onions in a tower, set them afire, and chop them into small pieces as they fell. Grinning, she looked over at Cruz, only to find his eyes trained on her. The look on his face, however, was no less enchanted than hers.

Without a word, his arm snaked around her waist and tugged her closer, as together, they leaned in and watched the rest of the cooking demonstration.

The meal was as impressive as the performance. "Dessert?" Cruz asked when they were done.

"How can you ask that? I couldn't even finish all my meal!" She moaned in mock agony, indicating the half-full plate she had shoved aside. "As it is, you may have to roll me out."

He chuckled and paid the bill, and then helped her into her jacket. As they stepped out into the cool night air, both were reluctant to see the evening end.

"How about a closer look at that fountain?" Cruz suggested.

"Excellent idea."

He took her hand as they wove their way toward the reflective pool. A crowd still gathered outside the door of the restaurant, awaiting their turn to get in.

"Looks like we beat the crowd and got here early," Cruz said. "I'm glad we weren't in line that long."

"I wouldn't have minded," Grace admitted shyly. It would have meant their date lasted longer.

Entwining his fingers with hers, he leaned close and confided, "Me, either."

They slowly circled the perimeter of the large pool, watching the lights dance upon the water. The night air was cool and brisk, and soon Cruz put his arm around her waist to keep them both warm. Away from the noise and bustle of University Drive and the foot crowds still spilling from the eateries, they found a quieter, less crowded view of the fountain. Their feet gradually slowed to a stop.

"I'm glad we did this, Grace." His voice was deliciously warm and deep.

"Me, too. I've enjoyed it."

"Joe tells me I should try the Italian restaurant next door, as well."

"Really? I haven't been there yet."

"Maybe we can go there when I come back in two weeks."

Grace tried to tone down the smile taking possession of her face. "I'll look forward to it."

"Speaking of Joe... I had no idea he lived in such a big house. Four bedrooms."

"Really? And it's just him?"

Cruz didn't answer immediately. When Grace glanced up at him, she was surprised to see the expression on his face. The big, strong man beside her looked oddly vulnerable, as if he were torn between hopefulness and dread.

"Yes. For now, anyway." Cruz was slow in answering,

adding, "He said he had considered looking for a roommate."

"I did hear a rumor about him and Dr. Sherwood..."

"Not a female." Cruz turned so that he was now facing her. His face was in the shadows, but she could still the reflection of light in his eyes. Or did that light come from within? Despite her impossibly full belly, there was still room for the swarming butterflies. "He offered a room to me."

Not daring to get her hopes up, Grace avoided his gaze as she asked, "And?"

"I told him I would think about it. It would depend on how my interview went."

Her eyes flew up to meet his. "Wait. Interview? You mean you..."

"Yes. I set up an interview for the job offer."

She couldn't help the smile that spread over her face. "You mean you may move back here?"

Cruz stepped closer, slipping his arm further around her waist. With the other hand, he cupped her cheek. "Oh, Grace," Cruz murmured, "I never wanted to leave in the first place."

Before she could ask any questions, he lowered his head to hers. And as their lips touched, all coherent thought fled from her mind. Wrapping her arms around his neck, Grace lost herself to the sheer glory of kissing this man. The man she had been in love with for almost half her life.

There was no reason to pretend otherwise. She was in love with Cruz Carlton. Always had been, always would be.

"Grace," he whispered, lips hovering over hers. His voice sounded oddly bereft. "I have no right... There's so much you don't know..."

"I know this wishing fountain really does work," she murmured back.

He laid his cheek against hers. She imagined it was to hide his eyes from her when he whispered in her ear. "I have demons, Grace."

"I know. But I can help you."

"The things I've seen. The things I've done." His voice was broken. When she felt him tremble, she slipped her arms beneath his bomber jacket for a heartfelt embrace.

"It's okay, Cruz," she purred. "You don't have to go through this alone. I can help you."

"You don't know the half of it. You don't know—"

She interrupted him with a tight squeeze of her arms. "And you don't have to tell me, not if you don't want to. But in time, when you're ready to talk, I'll be here for you."

After a moment of holding one another close, faces pressed together, Cruz lifted his head and gazed down at her.

"You have no idea how many times I've thought of you over the years," he told her. "How badly I wanted to see you again. To talk to you, like I used to."

Her throat was too tight to allow anything more than a simple, "I know," to escape.

"I'm sorry, Grace. If this truly were a wishing fountain, I would wish to go back and change the past. I would wish that night—"

Before he could finish the sentiment, a distinctive ringtone filled the night air. The haunting melody of Tchaikovsky's masterpiece as only Hope played it interrupted Cruz's words. Not wishing to be disturbed at such an inopportune moment—and certainly not by her sister—Grace fumbled in her pocket for her phone.

Her phone was dark, but the music continued to play. Confused, Grace looked up at Cruz.

And saw the truth in his eyes.

A thunderous frown darkened his face. *Of all times for Hope to call!* he thought angrily to himself.

Why hadn't he deleted her number from his phone? He ignored her last call and had no desire to ever speak to her again. *And why was she calling again, anyway?* She had no way of knowing he was here in College Station. She probably didn't even know he had been released from the Army. They had absolutely no reason to be in touch.

Knowing the damage was already done, Cruz didn't attempt to silence the ring. It stopped soon enough anyway, but not before Grace recoiled in horror.

"You—You've kept *in touch* with her?" she cried.

Cry was an apt word. There were no tears, not yet, but the pain and betrayal weighed heavy in her words. "All—All this time, you never said a word."

"There was nothing to say."

Grace shook his hands away. She stood back as if his nearness offended her. "You lied to me."

"I swear, I did not. I never lied to you, Grace."

"You did. You told me you hadn't kept in touch with her. And yet, your phone says differently. You even have her ringtone!"

"She sent it to me, along with her contact information," he defended himself. "When *she* reached out to me. Not the other way around."

"I find that hard to believe."

"It's the truth. I made the mistake of answering the

first time she called. It hasn't happened since."

"And I suppose it's just a coincidence that both of you are in town this weekend, and she just happens to call." He could hear the pain and betrayal in the words.

"Yes. A very unfortunate and inopportune coincidence, but yes." He reached for her, trying to make her understand. "Please, Grace. You have to believe me."

"Don't touch me!"

It was the coldness in her tone that gave Cruz pause. She wasn't hysterical. She wasn't crying. The cold, flat *nothingness* in her voice was far worse. It twisted his gut into a helpless knot.

Grace backed away another step. "I need to go home," she announced abruptly. When he started to move forward, she stopped with a splayed palm. "No. I'll call an Uber and get my own ride. I need to be alone right now."

"Absolutely not," Cruz ground out. "I brought you, I'll take you home."

"You don't understand. I can't look at you right now. Don't follow me."

With that, Grace turned and fled.

Stunned, Cruz was slow to respond. Those few seconds were all she needed to get a head start on him. A nearby restaurant was hosting live music on their patio, providing all the cover Grace needed to blend into the crowd. Cruz searched futilely all along the plaza, but he never found her.

He didn't even have her phone number. The only thing he knew to do was to drive back to her condo and plead for her to listen.

But even when he arrived, she refused to open the door. He had no way of knowing if she were even home, causing him more angst. What if there had been an accident? What if she had been mugged while waiting for the driver to arrive? What if—

Cruz felt a panic attack coming on. Grace was the most important person in his life, but this wasn't about him. The thought of something happening to her was unbearable. The thought of her being in danger physically was enough to drive him over the edge.

He needed to keep his wits about him. He had to keep calm. Practicing his deep-breathing techniques, he waited for the panic to abate before renewing his efforts of pounding on Grace's doorbell.

Once, he thought he heard movement from within. He started talking to the door, begging her to at least tell him she had made it home. After ten minutes with no response, he made one last attempt.

Forehead propped against the door, he resorted to groveling.

"Grace. I don't know your number. You won't answer me. You leave me with only one option. I don't know what else to do, but to call your sister. I don't want to. But unless you answer me and let me know you made it home safely, I'll go out of my head with worry. Calling Hope is my last resort. Please, please, just—"

A light went on in the foyer.

Relief sabotaged his knees, and Cruz sagged against the doorframe. She was safe.

It took a long moment before he realized she hadn't opened the door, hadn't given him a verbal confirmation. But she was safe, and that was what mattered.

"Thank you, Grace," he finally said. "I'll go now. I just needed to know you were home safely. I know you're still hurt; I know you don't want to talk to me, but you're safe, and that's what matters."

With one last mournful look at the door, Cruz turned and walked away.

CHAPTER TEN

Her heart broke all over again.

Back at the plaza, when she realized Cruz lied to her by omission, Grace felt as if he had stabbed her in the heart and left it bleeding. Knowing he had kept in contact with Hope—realizing she was still on the receiving end of her sister's hand-me-downs—was devastating.

But this.

Watching Cruz at her doorstep, seeing the pain and worry on his face, was heart wrenching. Grace's heart didn't just hurt. It felt ripped from her chest. She looked down to see if the damage were evident; surely, a pain so deep had to show!

The pain paralyzed her. She couldn't move. Her feet were like lead and her knees like gelatin. Grace was physically incapable of going forward and opening the door, even when hearing the raw desperation in his voice. How could she comfort him, when her own pain was so great?

It killed her, seeing Cruz in such a tortured state. He kept pushing his hands through the short stack of his hair, frantic to have her reply, to know that she was safe. She saw the lines of angst on his face, heard the desperation in his voice. Witnessed the onset of a panic attack.

Knowing he valued her safety over her forgiveness— his worry wasn't for himself; it was for *her*—was like a twist to the knife already penetrating her heart. Somehow, it made his betrayal even more painful. How could a man so caring and so unselfish be so blind to her sister's shallowness? Hope cared for only herself, and yet this wonderful man had chosen Hope over her, time and time again.

That one painful fact kept her immobile. Grace had no comfort to offer him. She had no words to give. Consumed by her own pain, the best she could do was turn on the light and let him know she was inside.

Even that exhausted her. Grace sank to the floor, still watching Cruz through the doorbell app on her phone.

Tears slipped down her cheeks as she watched the man she loved ultimately turn and walk away from her. Again.

Would she never learn?

Grace purged everything in her closet that was a hand-me-down from Hope. She had done the same thing a decade before, the first time Cruz walked away from her.

Back then, it had been a significant portion of her closet; bound by the limited means of a teenager, she had to take what she could get. That usually meant things that had once belonged to her sister. This time, however, there were only a few select pieces to discard. A floral dress that made Hope look 'washed out.' A ruffled skirt that made her look 'too hippy.' An evening gown she had already worn in public and couldn't be seen in again, Heaven forbid. A purse that was too big and bulky but too expensive to toss out. Even though it was also too ugly (despite the designer label it sported) for her to wear, Hope thought it was perfect for her sister. The same was said for a silk blouse and a tie-dye dress still dangling its tags.

Grace added the pair of black boots to the pile, the only item she regretted getting rid of. And, of course, there was the blue cashmere sweater from last night. That was *definitely* going in the discard pile! She wasn't offering the items back to her sister, either. She was donating them to the women's shelter this very afternoon, or as soon as she could summon the energy to take a shower and get dressed. So, maybe tomorrow. Monday, at the latest.

She knew it was a sign of defeat, but Grace couldn't assemble the effort to care. She was content to wallow in her misery; pajamas, ice cream, and all. It occurred to her that Hope might surprise her and actually try to see her new apartment. If the bowels of the earth froze over, she might even take Grace's suggestion of Sunday dinner with her father.

To be on the safe side and to assure a Hope-free weekend, Grace sent a pro-active text that said, *Lucky me. There was a stomach virus going around the hospital, and guess who caught it?* It wasn't a straight-out lie, but she knew it was enough to keep Hope miles away. Hope Stavenaugh would never be as undignified and uncouth as to succumb to a lowly stomach virus.

She switched her phone to silent and ignored any incoming calls and messages. As she suspected, none came from her sister, other than an expressive emoji that summed up their entire relationship.

It was late that evening before Grace looked at her phone again. An afternoon of sappy movies had her feeling lazy and entitled. Over a frozen pre-cooked meal—she didn't want to see a living soul, not even for food delivery—she scanned her phone for messages and alerts.

There were eight missed calls from the same unknown number. She instinctively knew they were from Cruz. After a lengthy argument with herself, (she wasn't sure if she came out the winner or the loser) Grace played them one by one.

"Hey. It's me. Cruz. Please don't hang up. I got your number from Joe, but don't be mad at him, or at anyone from the hospital for giving it up. I just want to talk to you... Grace? Are you there?"

"Hey. It's me. I really need to talk to you. Please, pick up the phone...."

"It's me again. Please, Grace. Please, talk to me. I can't stand the way things ended with us last night. It was such a perfect evening, until *she* called. I didn't call her back, Grace. You've got to know that. I've never called her back. I have nothing to say to your sister. It's you I want to talk to. Please, Grace. Talk to me."

Grace pushed away the half-eaten meal and went for the *real* comfort food. Pulling her cappuccino and a bag of Cheetos close, she played the fourth message.

"Ten years, Grace. That's how long I've waited to talk to you. I can wait a little longer, until you decide to. Pick. Up. This. Phone."

He waited a while before the next call.

"It's me. Again. Still waiting to talk to you. This is all a misunderstanding, Grace. If you'd just let me explain... Call me back."

By the next call, his patience had grown thin. "Pick up, Grace. I know I have the right number. I know you're ignoring me. I know you don't want to talk to me, but there's things that need to be said between us. Pick up the phone, Grace."

The firm tone in his voice dissolved by the seventh message. She heard a distinct catch in his words. "Please, Grace. This past week has meant so much to me. Please, please, *please* talk to me. I've missed you, Grace. I've missed *us*. Please, don't throw it all away. Talk to me."

Grace wasn't sure she wanted to hear the last message. The timestamp was from an hour ago.

"I can't leave town without one last try. Your friendship means the world to me. You have no idea how much I... Grace. Just talk to me. Just let me tell you how sorry I am for hurting you. I am so, so sorry. For last night, and for all those years ago... If you aren't ready to talk to me yet, I understand. I'll wait. I've waited for you this long; I can wait a little longer. But I need you in my life, Grace. You're the piece that's been missing.... Maybe we need this break. Maybe these two weeks will give us both time to sort things out and get our heads on straight. If you want to talk before that, all you have to do is call. Night or day, I'll talk to you. I'll drop what I'm doing, and I'll talk to you, by phone or in person. Whatever you want, whatever you need. Just don't shut me out.... So, I'll go now. I have some loose ends to tie up, but I swear, I will be back. Two weeks, Grace. I'll be back in two weeks, and one way or another, you and I are going to talk. Take care of yourself. Call if you need anything... Bye, my sweet Grace."

Two weeks seemed like an eternity. Grace was tempted to call him back, but she steeled herself to stay strong.

Maybe Cruz was right. Maybe they did need this time apart. After a ten-year separation, they had seen one another for four days straight. It was enough to send any heart into a flurry.

Maybe she needed this time to step back, re-evaluate her feelings, and ask herself what she really wanted.

I want Cruz, her heart whispered.

"I know that," she snapped aloud, her tone somewhat impatient. "The question is, *does he want you?* And are you strong enough to hear the truth, once and for all?"

To that, her heart had no comeback.

It turned out to be a productive weekend.

After wallowing in self-pity on Saturday, Grace put extra effort into her Sunday. By the end of the day, her walls were no longer bare, her closet wasn't the only thing purged and cleaned, all the laundry was done, and she even found time to go grocery shopping.

Staying busy kept her mind off Cruz and kept her from replaying his phone messages every few minutes. It also gave her a strategy for surviving the next two weeks. She signed up for extra shifts, committed to a continuing education course she had been putting off, attended a Meet'n Greet Mixer for tenants, and picked up a new suitor along the way.

In a weak moment, she agreed to go out with Dave, another newcomer to the complex. The young professor was nice looking, and they had a great deal in common, but her mind kept straying to Cruz.

Nothing new there. I've been thinking about Cruz for over a decade, she acknowledged.

But when he bent to kiss her that night, Grace shied

away. She liked knowing that Cruz's lips had been the last lips to touch hers. To his credit, Dave understood and asked for a second date, but Grace made no promises. She knew it wouldn't be fair to him. Her heart had been taken many years before.

Grace told herself she wasn't counting, but two weeks slipped into three. Had he changed his mind? Had he stood her up? Or was it a scheduling issue? She resisted the urge to ask Dr. Renaldi, and she refused to call Cruz. If he *had* changed his mind, she wouldn't beg him to reconsider.

She simply picked up more shifts, these on midnights. It wasn't her favorite way to spend a weekend, but it kept her busy and kept her from feeling sorry for herself.

Grace had just parked when her phone sang out Tchaikovsky's melody. After a brief hesitation, she picked up. It was best talking to her sister when no one else was around.

"Hello, Hope."

"I saw your text. What do you mean, you gave away my blue cashmere?"

Her indignation was almost comical. "You're rather late, dear sister. I sent that text almost two weeks ago."

"I just now read it."

Grace rolled her eyes and silently translated. *Code for 'your texts weren't important enough to read in a timely manner.'*

"I don't know what to say, Hope. I've already donated the items, and I'm sure they've been snatched up by someone who will love and appreciate them."

"Them? What else did you give away?" her sister snapped.

"Mmm, just a few things you handed down to me. Nothing you'll miss."

"I gave those things to *you*! You had no right to give

them away to someone else!"

"Of course I did," Grace said, keeping her voice calm and reasonable. "You *gave* them to me, making me the new owner. But don't worry. It counts as a taxable contribution, and I listed you as the donor. You get all the credit for the generous gesture."

"I should hope so! That sweater alone was worth a small fortune! I can only imagine what else you gave away."

"If you'd like to eliminate me as the middle-man, next time you can just give the items directly to the shelter," Grace offered.

"Please tell me you didn't just say a shelter," Hope said, her voice dripping with exaggerated horror. "As in some homeless woman roaming the streets in a five-hundred-dollar designer sweater?"

"I have no idea who the end recipient is. It could be a battered woman getting out of an abusive relationship, a single mother who's wearing it to a job interview, or someone wearing it for warmth because she has nothing else to keep her warm and dry, including a roof over her head. No matter, it's a kind and generous thing to do, and you weren't wearing the items to begin with," Grace pointed out.

"What has gotten into you, Grace? The last few times we've talked, you don't even sound like my sister!"

"I don't think that's it, Hope. I'm the same person I've always been. I think it's that you've never really taken the time to know me."

"Don't be ridiculous. Of course, I know you. We grew up together. We shared a bedroom. We shared a closet. And apparently, we even shared boyfriends."

Grace bristled. Was she referring to Cruz? "I'm not sure I would classify most of those things as *sharing*,"

Grace pointed out. "You had no choice on the room and the bed, and whenever you had friends over or were feeling particularly cranky, you kicked me to the floor. The other things were simply your hand-me-downs."

"I suppose you're referring to Julian," Hope said with a bored sigh. "It was hardly even a date. We met over drinks with friends. Obviously, he didn't make that big of an impression on me or I would have recognized his name when you first told me you were dating him. I'm not sure that counts as a hand-me-down, even though he was using you to get to me."

She no longer cared about Julian and his devious ways. Grace dared to ask the question weighing heavy on her heart.

"And Cruz?"

"Cruz? The boy who hung around me in high school? What about him?"

"Have you kept in touch with him through the years?"

"He went into the Air Force."

"Army," Grace corrected.

"Whatever." She could imagine Hope waving her manicured hand through the air in a gesture of nonchalance. To her sister, his years of service and sacrifice were insignificant. "Yes, we've spoken a time or two. He was in the news a while back, and my publicist suggested I reach out to him and renew our acquaintance."

"And did you?" Grace held her breath, waiting for the reply.

"I reached out, but he wasn't particularly receptive. If I recall correctly, he always was an odd duck. In fact, I think I remember the two of you getting along rather well together. Birds of a feather, and all..." she murmured, allowing the insult to float on the line between them.

Not that it mattered. Grace was no longer listening.

He was telling the truth! her heart sang. A huge smile broke out on her face.

"Hope, I just pulled in at work, and I really have to go. We'll talk later."

"I was just calling about the items I donated to charity."

Hope's mind had already spun the entire situation in her favor, making the donation all about her. If the conversation ever came up again, Hope would remember it as being her idea to donate the items to those 'poor, less fortunate souls.' She wouldn't forget to claim the tax deduction or the credit, either.

So typical. Grace shook her head as she walked to the employee entrance of the hospital. *So self-centered. So Hope.*

Maybe Cruz saw through her, after all. If what Hope said was true and he wasn't receptive to her calls, maybe he wasn't as blinded to her faults as Grace assumed. Maybe she owed him the benefit of the doubt.

"I wish I had asked Hope why she called him again that night," Grace muttered to herself as she opened her locker. "Probably couldn't stand the thought of a missed conquest."

Jana Torino turned from the locker next to her. "Are you talking to me?"

"No, sorry. Just having a conversation with myself."

"I'm surprised to see you here. Are you filling in for someone? I didn't see your name on the schedule."

"No, I called in and asked if there were any shifts available, and Nurse Lin said she had something open." Grace tamed her long blond strands into a ponytail. "So, here I am."

"We must have a full house, then. I've already seen several others check in."

"Game day weekend." She shrugged. "Anytime the Aggies play in town, we get extremely busy."

"I know that's right," her friend agreed. "I made the mistake of working the ER one game day last year. *Fandemoniums*, they call them. The food at the tailgate parties was fun, but you wouldn't believe some of the crazy cases that come into the ER on game day!"

Being in a busy college town that was home to one of the premiere universities in the nation, it wasn't just the restaurants and hotels that profited from SEC sports. The local hospitals saw their fair share of increased traffic, too.

"Yes, I would," Grace reminded her. "The worst ones end up here with us."

They walked together to the nurse's station to relieve the day staff, chatting along the way. The charge nurse was there to greet them.

"Grace? You'll be working on special assignment tonight," the ranking nurse informed her. "We have a patient in Room 259."

Grace tried not to look concerned. Room 259 was one of the two rooms used for Infectious Control, or, when needed, the Psych Ward. It featured an isolation cubicle and special lock-down features for a reason.

"Ooo-kay." She drew out the word.

"No need to look so worried," Nurse Lin assured her. "He seems harmless enough."

With a little laugh, Grace said, "Gee, thanks." Then she added, "I think."

"If it's not enough to keep you busy, I have some charting you can help with. And even in this computer age, there's always filing."

"And cranky old Mr. Blue is still here," one of the other nurses pitched in. "If you're in danger of falling asleep, you can have him." Obviously, the uncooperative patient was one of hers.

Grace held her palms up to stave off the generous offers. "I think I'll see what I'm up against, before I volunteer to take on anyone else."

"If it helps ease your mind, Martha volunteered to stay over. Her husband probably had other ideas about that, though," Nurse Lin chuckled.

Grace's heart ticked up a beat. Martha had openly ogled Cruz the day he warmed up for his physical endurance tests. Grace pushed her way through to the first computer she saw, eager to pull up the chart for Room 259.

A smile broke across her face when she saw the name Cruz Colton.

A frown quickly followed.

He hadn't called her to say he was in town. Did that mean he had changed his mind? Had he had time to think about what he wanted and decided it wasn't her?

There was only one way to find out, and only one thing to do. She was his nurse. It was her job to see to his physical well-being, no matter what their personal relationship may or may not be. She would let him set the mood for anything beyond her professional duties.

As he had only recently been admitted, there was no MAR, or medication administration record, to review. Grace tended to a few non-pressing issues before she made the trek down to the corner room.

As she stepped into the isolation cubicle and washed up, she saw Dr. Renaldi already there, doing the same.

"Hello, Grace," he said in his rich baritone.

"Hi, Doc," she responded. She wondered if he had

requested her as a nurse this evening, or if it were all a coincidence. She nodded to the sealed, disposable gowns on the counter. "Do I need to suit up for infectious reasons?"

"Nah. We're just using this room because it gets lonely down here in the corner," he said with a smile. "That, and because it's quiet. Our patient will be staying awake all night." He winked as he pushed the inside door connecting to the patient room.

Grace heard the men exchange hearty greetings. She took a deep breath of courage and stepped forward into the room.

"Grace." Cruz sounded surprised. Was that a hint of pleasure in his words, as well?

She was proud of her voice for coming out so steady. "Hello, Cruz. I see you've come back for another round of Doc's special care." Instead of allowing her eyes to devour the man in the chair—*and, oh man, he looked even more handsome this time than before, if that were even possible!*—she turned her eyes on the doctor.

"Is that what you're calling it now?" Cruz drawled.

"It sounds better than what you call it," Joe Renaldi said with an easy grin.

"And who, better than I, would know all about torture techniques?"

Instead of laughing, the physician had a serious look on his face. Grace's eyes flew to Cruz. She saw the same expression there in his face.

Worry gathered on her brow. Had Cruz been tortured during the war? Her heart ached at the thought.

"So!" Joe broke the tension with the booming word, punctuated by a clap of his hands. "I need to give you both a brief rundown of this evening's festivities. Our patient here has been awake since midnight. Correct?"

When Cruz confirmed the claim with a nod, the doctor continued.

"Our goal this weekend is to keep him awake for as long as possible. This is a study of how sleep deprivation affects a person's reaction time, reflexes, cognitive function, and physical endurance. Grace, your primary focus tonight will be to keep our patient awake. In the morning, we'll run a battery of tests. We'll repeat the entire scenario tomorrow night and again the next morning and compare both results to tests I performed when he was here on his last visit. Any questions?"

"I'm assuming he won't be allowed to sleep any tomorrow, either?" She knew it was in the name of science, but it seemed rather harsh.

"Nothing the Army hasn't required of him before, I can assure you," the doctor said. "We'll cap this experiment at fifty-four to sixty hours. He can sleep after we conclude tests around noon on Sunday."

Grace darted a glance at Cruz. "And you're okay with this?"

"I'm here of my own volition," Cruz assured her, his voice dry. She thought she saw a glimmer of gratitude in his eyes, however.

"Just checking," she muttered.

"He'll get a little grumpy," Joe predicted, "but he'll never be in any physical danger. If he shows signs of obvious distress—which I am sure he won't—we'll stop the experiment immediately. But your concern is noted and appreciated."

"I assume I'll take his vitals, as I would with any patient?"

"Yes. You can use any natural means you wish to keep him alert and awake, including exercise, mind stimulation, and taking walks outside the hospital. Within designated areas, of course."

"Of course."

"For tonight, we'll limit the use of caffeine stimulation to 400 mg. Tomorrow night, we may consider over-the-counter stimulants, such as soldiers might use during maneuvers."

"I thought we weren't torturing him," Grace mumbled.

"Again, I appreciate your concern, but he'll be under close supervision the entire time," Joe reminded her. He mentioned a few additional things before bidding them good night and good luck.

Then, it was just the two of them in the room.

CHAPTER ELEVEN

"It sounds like we have a busy night ahead," Grace commented. Hardly the stuff of brilliance, but it was better than the silence that had settled between them.

"It would seem."

"On the bright side, I shouldn't get sleepy on my shift," she reasoned. "Not if I'm keeping you awake."

"We can only hope."

His short, stilted answers reminded Grace of his first visit to the hospital. That was the first time she realized the boy she once knew had changed a great deal during their decade apart. Her insides rearranged themselves into a knot.

"Are you good for an hour or so? I need to help some of the other nurses with their load." Technically not true, but she felt suddenly stifled in a room with just the two of them.

"I should be good for several hours," he predicted.

"I won't be that long, but good. I'll check back in when it's time to take your vitals."

She almost made it to the door when he called her name.

"Yes?" she asked, turning back.

His dark eyes warmed her from across the door. His voice was low, but she could distinctly hear the words. "It's good to see you again."

Relief flooded through her. She didn't trust her voice to speak, so she nodded and quickly left the room.

True to his word, the monitors showed Cruz had no problems staying awake as the clock ticked toward midnight. Grace used the time to help her co-workers with their patient loads and—even if she were reluctant to admit it—to gather her courage. Sooner or later, she knew she would have to spend more than five minutes in his presence.

Around eleven, she brought him a high protein snack and a glass of orange juice.

"No coffee?" he asked, brow arched.

"I thought we might grab that on our walk."

"So, if I'm a good boy and eat all my dinner, I get a reward?" The curled corner of his mouth softened his sardonic tone.

Her smile was more obvious, stretching to both corners of her mouth. "Something like that."

"Then hand over that peanut butter."

As Cruz ate his snack, Grace tidied his room. When she saw a copy of *The Shack* lying on his bedside, her smile returned. So, he had taken her advice and gotten the book.

Just for a moment, it felt like old times.

"Do you have a jacket?" she asked. "I thought we could stroll through the courtyard, but there's a nip in the air. It may be too cool for a t-shirt." She nodded to the gray one he wore over sweatpants.

"I have a hoodie in the closet."

Grace retrieved the hoodie—also Army-issue gray—and tossed it to him as he finished his snack.

Ever the gentleman, he paused in pulling it over his head and asked, "Do you need this?"

"Thanks, but I have a sweater. I'll grab it on the way down."

As they walked through the quiet hallway, Grace couldn't help but notice the appreciative looks her companion drew from the other nurses. A solitary female patient, strolling the corridors while battling insomnia, stopped after passing them and enjoyed the view from the backside. Grace wanted to protest on Cruz's behalf, but he seemed oblivious to the stir he created. Maybe he was accustomed to women ogling him.

She stopped to get her sweater and accepted Cruz's offer to help slip it on. Did she imagine it, or was that a light caress as his hands lingered? He wasn't sending very clear signals tonight. One moment he was curt, the next moment he was courteous.

I hope his next job isn't as an air traffic controller. What a mess that would be!

She must have chuckled at the thought, because Cruz looked at her sharply, brows arched in silent question.

Grace waved off the attention. "Ignore me."

She thought she heard him grunt, "Impossible."

They stopped for coffee before she led him through a small sitting area just off the church chapel. A door opened into the night and the small courtyard beyond. Cool air swirled around them, biting against their skin.

Pulling his hood over his neck, Cruz hunched his shoulders to eliminate a gap around his neck. "You weren't kidding about that nip in the air. It's gotten cooler since I came in."

"It *is* late October in the South," she reminded him. "Warm days, cool nights." She struck a cutie pose and drawled, "It's fall, y'all."

Her antics drew a smile. Perhaps as a reward, he offered a tiny piece of information about himself. "That was one of the best things about the two years I was stationed in Massachusetts. They actually *have* fall."

It was the opening she had hoped for. As they followed the tiled path woven between colorful fall plants and neatly trimmed box shrubs, Grace sipped from her coffee and dared to ask, "Will you tell me about it?"

"Massachusetts?"

"No. The Army." Hearing his sharp intake of breath, she rushed to say, "You heard the doctor. He said to use natural means to keep you awake. He specifically mentioned exercise and mental stimulation. In my book, that means walk and talk."

"Try a different book," he all but growled.

Her tone was gentle as she admonished him. "You heard his parting words, same as I did. He said I was the boss, and you were to do as I said." Her voice softened even more. "Please, Cruz. I'd like to know about your life over the past ten years."

"It may not be a very pretty tale. May even give you nightmares." Just under his breath, he added, "It does me."

"I'll be up all night, remember? Right here alongside you."

Grace didn't push. Before they reached the end of the first lap, Cruz began talking.

"If I had to be stuck up North, Cape Cod definitely the place to be. The shoreline was incredible. It's different from our beaches along the Gulf. Even the salt air has a different taste to it."

He told her about the sandy beaches and the breezes coming across Nantucket Sound. Grace had been there as a teenager—naturally, the trip was tied to Hope's concert in Boston—but never as an adult. She thought she would like to go back, especially after hearing his vivid descriptions.

Cruz talked at length about the Joint Base where he had been stationed. It was home to five military commands that trained for missions at home and overseas, conducting airborne search and rescue missions, and intelligence command and control. Joint Base Cape Cod was where he started his MOS as instructor for Search and Rescue. From there, he moved on to teach SAR in Missouri, Arizona, and Texas. His last base had been Ft. Hood, practically in their own backyard.

Knowing Cruz had been only two hours away at Ft. Hood and never reached out to her brought a new ache to Grace's heart, but she kept her sorrow to herself. Cruz was finally talking, and it was the best form of therapy she could hope for. Not just for tonight, but for his mental well-being in general.

She only interrupted him to clarify things she didn't understand, such as the term MOS. He explained it meant Military Operational Specialty.

"Why search and rescue?" she asked softly, stopping to ditch their empty cups as they neared a trashcan.

His answer was slow in coming. Hunching further into his hoodie, Cruz's voice was low when he spoke. The words, when they came, had a raw edge to them. "I, uh, had personal experience with how... crucial it can be."

She moved closer to him as they made another round.

Close enough that he could feel her warmth. Close enough to hear her soft encouragement. "I'd like to hear about it, if you'd like to tell me."

He didn't *want* to tell her.

But he needed to.

Cruz was tired of the walls that stood between them. He was tired of lies and half-truths, and lingering ties to the past. He wanted to start over and start fresh.

"We were stationed in Iraq."

He began the tale in his raspy, pensive voice. The oppressive subject added unneeded weight to words already heavy with pain and reflection. He told her about fighting the enemy and the harshness of war. He glossed over the worst of it, reluctant to put the horrific images in her head. His voice faltered as he described that fateful day, the day he chose to save the lives of innocent children over his own.

He didn't put it that way, of course. He downplayed any heroism on his part, but Grace read between the lines. She circled her hands around his sinewy arm, silently offering her support as he struggled through the difficult words.

"And then I was falling." His voice broke a bit, and she hugged his arm closer. He acknowledged her presence, but he wouldn't be distracted. He was determined to power through. "Down, down, down." With each word, his voice scraped lower, raking against the pit of his heart. "The ground rushed up to meet me, and there was this terrible, deafening racket. The sound of breaking limbs and twisting metal and all kinds of warning bells and sirens. I heard someone scream in agony."

His leg faltered as if in memory. They came to a stop in the courtyard, but the past moved on before his eyes.

Cruz stared blindly into the night, seeing the awful images again.

"There was smoke. It was all around me, choking me, blurring my vision." He reached out his free hand to wave through the thick haze only he could see. "I knew I had to get out of the aircraft, but I couldn't move. My leg was pinned in the carnage. It—It was my voice I heard screaming. I had never felt such agony in my life."

Grace bit back a sob.

"Someone… pulled me… from the wreckage." The words seemed pulled from him, even now. He swallowed hard as he stared into the darkness, literally and figuratively. "Dragged me. Over the ripped metal and the burning rubbish, and across the rocks and dirt. I passed out somewhere along the way and woke up in… a cave. A dark, damp, secluded cave." If possible, his voice fell even lower. "Where I spent the next two months."

A gasp escaped her. "Two months! You were…?" She couldn't bring herself to say the words.

"Yes," he confirmed. His voice was oddly flat. "I was a prisoner of war."

"Cruz." Once more, her heart felt ripped from her chest. The pain was for him and all that he had suffered. "Oh, Cruz." Hot tears fell from her eyes as she pressed her face against his arm.

"They left me there with tepid water and stale bread, brought once a day. They kept me from bleeding out, but offered nothing more than dirty bandages, changed every few days."

"How did you—how did you get out?"

The answer was simple. "Joe. Joe saved me."

She squeezed tighter, saying a prayer of thanks for his friend. No wonder Cruz gladly participated in these experiments. He truly did owe his life to Dr. Renaldi.

Cruz's feet began to move again. Grace saw it as a good sign. He needed to keep moving forward. He needed to walk away from the past and the horrors he had endured.

Grace fell into step beside him, her fingers still linked around his arm. The more they walked, and the more he talked, she felt some of the tension slip from his tightly coiled body.

"By the time they got to me, my leg was badly infected. I spent the next two months in the hospital. There was a point…" His voice faltered, but he forced himself to continue. "They almost took my leg," he confided in a low voice. "Joe fought for me. He was still a medic then, but he challenged the attending physicians and made them listen. If not for him, they would have amputated. If not for him, they may never have found me in the first place. I owe everything to Joe."

"What a wonderful testament to friendship," Grace murmured.

"He's more than my friend. He's my hero."

She gave his arm a squeeze as she whispered, "Mine, too, now."

They walked in silence for a few moments, until Cruz commented on the space where they tread. The change in subject was subtle, but Grace understood his need to step away from the darkness and focus on the present.

"I didn't realize this courtyard was even here," he said.

Beside him, Grace nodded. He suddenly resented his sweatshirt, wishing he could feel the silk of her hair against his bare arm. The scent of lemons filled his nostrils.

"It's our little hidden gem," she agreed. "Perfect for

quiet reflection."

He tilted his head to the side to touch hers, dark resting against light. "And midnight strolls."

"That, too." She smiled, snuggling closer against him.

They spoke of non-sequential things as the minutes slipped quickly away. When their legs tired and their skin chilled unmercifully against the night breeze, they left the quiet garden and returned to the second floor.

Grace checked in with the desk but when she came to his room again, it was with hot chocolate for them both. After she took his vitals, they settled on the couch, and she produced a game of chess.

They had been playing for a half hour when Cruz volunteered his thoughts on how military maneuvers were like the game; it was all about strategy and anticipating the move of your opponent. He talked about some of his missions, keeping the details sparse and the information declassified, but Grace knew the casual conversation was therapeutic for him. She gladly listened, offering minimal interruption as he willingly opened up about the painful past.

There was only one subject they didn't broach. Neither spoke of that last night when they were teenagers. By the time Cruz claimed checkmate, the sun had crawled its way into the sky, and there was movement in the hallway, signaling the turn of shift.

"I feel guilty, knowing I'm about to go home and get some rest, when you have to stay up all day," Grace admitted as she gathered the chess pieces and stored them into their box.

"Part of it," he assured her. "One of us needs to be fresh and alert for tonight's rematch."

"Just don't use exhaustion as an excuse *when I beat you*," she teased, leaning forward as she emphasized the words.

He tapped the end of her nose in a playful gesture. Grace abruptly sat back, blinking in surprise, as he said, "As long as you don't pretend to have given me the advantage *when I mop you across the board again.*"

Her heart thrilled at this playful side of him. Grace stood and assured him in sprightly jest, "You, sir, are *ON.*"

The twinkle in his eyes matched hers. "I'll look forward to it."

For someone who had stayed up all night, Grace felt amazingly fresh as she floated down the hall, still warmed by that sparkle.

CHAPTER TWELVE

Despite feeling optimistic when she left the hospital, Grace didn't sleep well that day. Her new bedroom allowed too much light in for optimal daytime sleeping, so she hung a blanket over the window to help darken the space. While that helped, her mind fought against her weary body and kept replaying the night's events and some of the secrets Cruz had shared. She was flattered he trusted her enough to open up and offer her this insight into his past.

He had worried sharing the realities of war might give her nightmares, but when she finally fell asleep, it wasn't his military stories that haunted her dreams. She kept reliving *that* night, the one that had preyed upon her for ten years.

She was dressed in her finery, a formal she had siphoned from Hope's side of the closet. The blue chiffon was a perfect fit for her own tall, willowy frame so like her sister's. The color was perfect for her, too. Grace had even managed to arrange her hair into a semblance of artful curls and long tresses.

Hope was getting dressed in their parents' room, where their mother helped her into an elaborate gown purchased especially for the senior prom. Neither had an inkling that Grace planned to attend. She was but a lowly sophomore, after all, and could only go as a senior's date. It never occurred to them that such a thing could happen.

As expected, a long stream of hopeful suitors had invited Hope to the dance, but she had held out for an invitation by one special boy. It was slow in coming, but Gregg Tomasek eventually broke up with his on-again/off-again girlfriend and asked Hope to the prom. Mother and daughter were so ecstatic that they never thought to wonder if Grace had been invited.

In truth, the invitation came as a shock to her, too.

After realizing Cruz was another of her sister's hand-me-downs, Grace had avoided any further contact with him. She ignored his calls and pretended she wasn't home when he dropped by the house. He attempted to seek her out at school, but she deftly avoided him there, as well. Cruz finally resorted to leaving her a note in the mailbox, addressed like a proper letter. When her father gathered the mail and delivered the envelope to her room, he never noticed the stamp hadn't been canceled.

The message had been brief.

"Grace Stavenaugh, will you do me the honor of attending Senior Prom with me? I know it's impossibly short notice, but I hope you'll accept. I'll pick you up at seven o-clock sharp. Please say yes. Yours always, Cruz Colton."

Thrilled beyond measure, she immediately went to the closet and ferreted out a dress. Two days was pathetically short notice, but Hope had more formals than Grace had jeans. She knew she could find the perfect dress in the crowded space, and she did.

Now she wore the gown and was minutes away from all her dreams coming true. She had a date with Cruz!

As the clock neared seven, Hope returned to their bedroom. She was too surprised to see Grace dressed for prom to realize she wore a borrowed gown. Besides, she had bigger things to worry about. Gregg hadn't returned any of her calls, and he was already five minutes late. They had pictures scheduled with a professional photographer in twenty minutes.

The telephone rang.

And the real nightmare began.

Rousing herself from sleep, it took a full moment for Grace to realize the ringing came from her phone and wasn't an echo from the past. She fumbled around for her cell, wondering if the interruption had spared her from reliving the worst of the nightmare. Again.

"What took you so long to answer? This is your mother, by the way."

"Yes, I still recognize your voice." Frogged with sleep, her unamused quip came out gruffer than she intended.

Suzanne Stavenaugh expressed her disapproval with a sniff. "I'm surprised that you do. You haven't called in ages."

"The phone rings both ways, Mom."

"Yes, and you see who's doing the calling now."

Grace didn't have the time or the inclination to play her mother's head games. "Was there a reason for your call? I was sleeping."

"In the middle of the day? Whatever is wrong with you? Hope said you've been acting strange lately, and she's right!"

"I'm working midnights this weekend, Mom. It's the only time I can sleep."

Suzanne paused long enough to consult a clock. "Well, it's almost five, so you may as well get up now. You'll need to take a shower and do something with that hair of yours."

Most people called her hair long and luxurious, marveling over the golden highlights and the silky texture. Somehow, her mother always made it feel as coarse and unattractive as a frayed rope.

"Hope says she loaned you a dozen outfits and you gave them all away to charity. While I find that in incredibly bad taste, I understand you were at least thoughtful enough to put them under her name. I'll need you to bring me the receipts so we can take the appropriate deductions."

"She didn't loan them to me. She gave them to me. She wrapped two of them as presents, even though they were obviously pre-worn. But, yes, I did give them away, and I did donate them under her name. When I come across the receipt, I'll take a picture and text it to you."

"I prefer a physical receipt."

"Then you can see my new apartment when you drop by to pick it up."

Grace heard the excuse in her mother's voice. "I've been so busy lately… I was hoping you could bring it here. I'll be home this evening, if you want to bring it before work."

Grace had learned the art of making excuses from Suzanne. "Like you said, I'll have to do something with this hair…"

"So maybe tomorrow?"

"Maybe."

To her surprise, Suzanne didn't hang up immediately. She even spoke of something other than her favored child. After a halfway pleasant chat with her mother, Grace gave up on sleep and lumbered to the shower.

With an impish smile, Grace knew she still had to do something with that hair of hers.

Cruz was too polite to mention the dark smudges beneath her eyes. Grace was reluctant to admit it, but he looked more refreshed than she did, even without benefit of sleep. As the clock neared midnight, she felt a flair of resentment against him. How could he still be so alert after forty-eight hours, and look so devastatingly handsome? Where were the dark circles, the drooping eyelids? His day-old beard and drawn features simply added to his rugged masculinity.

It's just not fair! she bemoaned. *Five hours of sleep and I look like death warmed over. No sleep at all, and he still looks as good as ever.*

She grabbed the chessboard and plopped it down between them, taking her frustrations out on the innocent game.

"That worried about taking on the champion?" he teased.

"In your dreams," she snorted.

"Speaking of dreams, how did you sleep?" He asked the question innocently enough, but she heard the subtle accusation in his voice.

Her reply was sharp. "Go ahead and mention them."

"Mention what?"

"The bags hanging from my eyes. We both know they're there. We both know I didn't sleep worth a dime."

Cruz placed the chess pieces in their appropriate squares, barely glancing up as he asked, "Why was that?"

Grace could have given the excuse of the sun streaming through her windows. She could have given the excuse of her mother calling and waking her. She could have cited a disrupted schedule or too much stimulation the night before. All were partially true. But none was the real culprit, and none was the whole truth.

Grace was tired of half-truths. She was tired of being haunted by the past and not knowing what really happened ten years ago. After their walk in the courtyard last night, they had reached a new intimacy in their relationship, but the invisible wall of the past still stood between them. Like Cruz, she needed to confront the demons of her past in order to move forward.

She paced across the room before she whirled and demanded, "Do you really want to know?"

Her blazing eyes captured his attention. Setting down the chess piece at random, his gaze leveled with hers. "I asked."

"I kept having a nightmare."

A frown moved across his face. "I knew I shouldn't have told you about the war!" Cruz chided himself for the poor lapse in judgment.

"It wasn't the war that kept me awake, Cruz. Not that war. It was my own internal war. The one I've had with myself for the last ten years." Her voice dropped, but she kept the distance of the room between them. "The one where I wonder what really happened that night, and why I can't just let it go. The war I've fought for a decade, wondering why I still care, when you so obviously didn't."

"Nothing could be further from the truth, Grace," he corrected her in his raspy voice. He stood abruptly, toppling the chessboard. The chess pieces scattered and rolled on the ground, but he paid them no heed as he moved toward the window and stared through the drawn shade. A pawn bounced and rolled under the bed, chased by a queen.

Had she noticed, Grace would have likened it to her life. She had never been more than a pawn in her sister's kingdom.

Unshed tears blazed in Grace's hazel eyes and gave her the courage to step forward. Each word was an accusation.

"Ten years, Cruz. That's how long I've waited. That's how long I've wondered what went wrong that night. Why you betrayed me and took my sister to the prom, instead of me. Was that your intention all along?"

He whirled to face her. "What? Of course not! How can you ask that?"

"Because that's what happened. You asked *me* to go, yet you left with her."

His reply seemed choked from him. "I had no choice."

Grace was disappointed in him for offering such a flimsy excuse. "There's always a choice, Cruz," she told him, her voice sad.

He surprised her by agreeing. "You're right, of course. But I was young and foolish. At that moment, I didn't think I had another option."

Grace closed her eyes, seeing it all again in her mind.

Hope was still screeching from the dining room, something about Gregg and 'that tart.' She was going to rip the other girl's hair out, one fake blond strand at a time. Gregg's eyes were doomed to a far more painful fate.

From what Grace could piece together, the phone call was from Gregg, informing Hope he had made up with his girlfriend and was taking Tiffany to the prom, instead of her. Rejection was such a foreign concept to her sister; she truly had no idea of how to cope with it. The sounds of Hope's meltdown almost drowned out the sound of the doorbell ringing.

Grace stepped from the bedroom, but her mother answered the door before she could maneuver the hallway in two-inch heels. The door opened and Cruz was there, filling the space with his dark good looks and his crisp tuxedo.

Grace's knees went weak at the sight of him. His dark eyes searched the room, stopping when they landed upon her, frozen there in the hall. A smile started in his eyes and spread to his face, and for a moment, it was just the two of them in the world.

It was difficult to hear over Hope's wails, but she saw Cruz's mouth move. He must have asked for her. From the corner of her eye, Grace saw her mother's head jerk up from her tissues. Though she handled the situation with more dignity than her daughter did, Suzanne was equally crushed by Gregg's untimely rejection. The tears streaming down her face were testament to the pain she felt, as keenly as if it were her own. Almost in slow motion, Suzanne turned and searched for her younger daughter.

Shifting her gaze to meet her mother's, Grace recalled the look of utter surprise in her mother's eyes.

But worse, far worse, was the calculating expression that quickly took its place.

The memory slammed into Grace like a runaway medical cart.

Why had she never remembered that before? What did it mean?

"You... My mother—my mother pulled you aside," Grace sputtered in realization. "One minute you were in the doorway, and the next she was dragging you to the kitchen. And then—and then..." She didn't have the strength to finish the thought while standing. She dropped abruptly onto the couch, her voice dazed. "And then you came back out, and you wouldn't even look at me. You—You left. With her. With Hope."

Cruz pushed his hand through his short hair. "Not a day has gone by that I haven't regretted my foolishness," he admitted in a raw voice. "I should never have left, but I knew you wouldn't understand. *I* didn't understand. I left as quickly as I could, because I couldn't bear to see the look of betrayal in your eyes. The hatred."

Grace quietly corrected him. "I never hated you."

"Then I hated myself enough for both of us," he told

her vehemently. He turned to pace the room, clearly agitated. He kept running his hand over his head. "I didn't want to. I knew it was wrong. I—I felt like scum. Lower than scum. But I didn't know what else to do."

Grace watched him pace the room, reminded of the night he paced in front of her apartment. He was clearly tortured by the decision he had made, ten years hence. Compassion warred in her heart with resentment. How different their lives would have been, if he had made a different choice that night!

In the end, her compassionate nature won. That, and her love for this man.

"You were barely eighteen," she reminded him in a soft voice. "You were raised to respect your elders. I never realized it before now, but my mother made you do it, didn't she? She took you aside, and she insisted that you take Hope to the prom. She probably told you that I would have other chances, but that this was Hope's only senior prom. It simply wouldn't do for the queen of the senior class to have been stood up by her date, so my mother convinced you to take Gregg's place."

A tear she didn't know she cried trekked down her cheek. Grace summed up her statement with a simple, "You did as you were told."

"How can you—how can you sit there and sound so calm?" Cruz stared at her in a mixture of gratitude and horror. It was a relief knowing that she understood, that she didn't hate him as much as he had hated himself all these years, but he couldn't imagine her acceptance. Thunderclouds gathered in his eyes.

"Your own mother sold you out! She knew *you* were my date for prom, but she forced me to take your sister, instead. She said she would..." He stopped himself before he caused Grace even more pain. She didn't need to know how Suzanne had all but blackmailed him, threatening to start horrible rumors about his character if he didn't agree to her scheme. "How can you just accept the way she treated you, and not be furious?"

Grace didn't quite meet his eyes. "I gave up being furious a long time ago," she said with frank honesty. "In her own way, my mother loves me, but she's… shallow. I'm not proud of the fact, but my mother is as shallow and selfish as my sister. Both are incapable of loving anyone else as much as they love themselves. Even though it hurts, I've learned to accept that fact."

"But… But she put Hope first!" he stuttered in outrage. "She didn't think of what it would do to you!"

"She has always put Hope and her needs first. She always will. That's just the sad truth, and it's the reason my parents are no longer married." Without making excuses for her mother, Grace tried explaining it in a way that Cruz could understand.

"Hope makes my mother look good. She makes her feel good about herself and her accomplishments as a parent. And for that, my mother loves and needs Hope in a way she can never love or need me."

Stunned by her quiet acceptance of the matter, Cruz stared down at her. "But that makes no sense. You're by far a better person than your sister! You're honest and intelligent and compassionate, and you have more integrity than your sister could ever hope to have. *You're* the one she should be most proud of!"

Cruz all but fell onto the couch beside her, clearly confused by the dynamics of the Stavenaugh family.

Grace managed a smile. "I appreciate that," she whispered. She wiped away the tears that continued their slow journey down her cheek. "But my mother values outer beauty more than she does inner strength. It's always been that way. I've come to love and accept my mother—and sister— for who and what they are, flaws and all."

"You may have had your entire life to get used to that," he told her, "but I couldn't handle it. I wanted no part of it. I—I couldn't stand to look at myself in the mirror. I couldn't stand the thought of running into your mother in town, or into your sister at school. I was sickened at the sight of her. She was nothing but a shallow, fickle, self-centered..." He stopped himself from completely berating Grace's sister. There was no need. Grace knew how she was.

He started over, his voice dropping. "Most of all, I couldn't bear the thought of running into you, knowing what I knew. Knowing I had failed you."

Grace looked at him in surprise. "Failed me?"

"You deserved so much better than that, but instead of standing up for you, I bailed. I signed up for the Army and left that very day." He ran his hand over his head again.

Grace recognized the signals of an oncoming panic attack. She reached up and grabbed his hand, forcing it down to his lap. She then held it with both her own, scooting closer to him.

"Cruz," she said in a soft, firm voice. "Look at me. It wasn't your fault."

"How can you say that?" His eyes met hers, then darted away again. "I ran away! I ran away and left you. I was in love with you, and I just left you behind." A wild look came into his eyes. "Joe should have done the same thing to me. After what I did to you, I didn't deserve to be rescued!"

There were so many things she should have said. She

should have argued with his failed logic. She should have reasoned with him. She should have talked him off the ledge.

Instead, she dissolved into a ridiculous puddle of warmth.

"You—You were in love with me?" she whispered.

The wonder in her voice caught his attention. He shifted his focus, forgetting for the moment about his own bout of panic.

"Of course, I was in love with you! *You* were the one I came to see. Did you really think my timing with Hope was that terrible?"

A shy smile touched her lips. "You did seem to have terrible luck catching my sister at home."

"I thought—I hoped—you felt the same. I was planning to ask you to prom, to be my girlfriend, but you suddenly shut me out. I didn't understand what happened, but I knew I had one chance to sweep you off your feet. I had this whole romantic night planned. I was going to read you an excerpt I found in a book, and I was going to tell you how I felt. But then..." He pulled one hand away, running it over his head again.

Grace leaned in, forcing him to look at her. "I did feel the same," she told him. "I was in love with you, too."

"Then why did you shut me out?"

She dropped her eyes to study their clasped hands. "Like you, I was young and foolish. I let pride get in my way."

"Pride? I don't understand."

She struggled to articulate her reasons. "Like most younger siblings, at least half of my clothes were hand-me-downs. Many of my favorite toys were Hope's, before they were mine. I know that's just how families work. I was probably more fortunate than most younger sisters, because Hope had some truly beautiful clothes, and lots of them. But sometimes—and I'm not proud to admit this, but it's true—sometimes, I just wanted something that was my very own."

"That, I understand," he murmured.

"Even though you first came to the house to see *her*," Grace continued, "I came to think of you as my very own. You were my secret fantasy. My perfect dream." She was too caught up in the past to be embarrassed by her honest admission. "But Hope being who she is, she found a way to ruin it for me. She loves reminding me, even now, that the clothes and the toys are really hers, and she's merely being gracious enough to share with me."

The blue sweater was an excellent case in point, but Cruz didn't know that. When Grace stole a look at his face, she knew he understood. His mouth was set in a grim frown.

"She tainted my dream of you," Grace confessed. "Of us. She pointed out that you were just another of her hand-me-downs."

"You thought I was using you to get to her?" He looked more worried than he did insulted.

"Insecurity can be an evil thing," Grace conceded. "It makes you doubt things you know are true, even yourself. And yes, in a moment of incredible insecurity and pride, I doubted that your interest in me was sincere. My beautiful dreams were crushed, destroyed by my sister's unique way of making me feel small and insignificant."

Cruz turned his hand so he could curl his fingers around hers. Sorrow laced his words. "And then I all but confirmed your worst fears by taking your sister to the prom, instead of you."

It shouldn't have smarted so, but it did. Still, after all these years.

"You know what?" Grace said, forcing a brave smile through the tears that were so determined to fall. "That was a decade ago. It's time we both put that behind us."

"But we wasted ten years! Ten years that we could have been together."

Sniffing back the tears, Grace twisted her lips in contemplation. "I prefer not to think of those years as wasted. It gave us both time to grow and mature, and to become the people we are today."

New warmth moved into his voice, smoothing out some of the raspy tones. "It also gave us time to know what we really want in life."

Her smile was hopeful. "Like a new career, here in College Station?"

"Yes. Like a new career, right here in College Station. Where my roots are." His hands tightened around hers. "Where you are."

Her heart dared to take flight. "You're coming home?"

Cruz nodded, his eyes alight with a special glow. "I'm coming home."

Grace touched her mouth to his, grazing his lips with the hint of a kiss. "What took you so long?" she asked in a whisper. She spoke the words lightly, not expecting a serious reply.

Yet when he answered, his voice was raw. "When I was captured, I thought it was God's way of punishing me for deserting you. I thought I deserved it." She made a sound of protest, until he shushed her. "I was a coward for leaving, but I decided dying would be the ultimate easy way out. So, I hung on. The entire time I was in there, I thought of you. I replayed every conversation, every accidental touch of your hand against mine, every expression to cross your beautiful face. You, Grace, gave me the courage and willpower to hang on, and to make it through those darkest days."

"I'm so glad you hung on," she whispered back, her voice as zealous as his.

Mere inches separated them. She could still feel the tension in his body. She knew he wasn't finished saying what he needed to say, so she waited.

"I hung on because of you, Grace," Cruz went on. "But, like you, insecurities set in. I didn't know if you'd want to see me. I wasn't sure I was welcome, so I stayed away. I convinced myself you were better off without me."

Grace heard the cloud of doubt still hanging over his heart, shrouding his confidence. His vulnerability was her undoing. Slipping her arms around his neck, she murmured, "Crazy talk."

She felt the tension leak from his body. His arms came up to circle her waist. "I know I have issues," he murmured against her mouth, "but calling me crazy is a bit harsh, don't you think?"

With only a whisper of breath between them, she felt the curl of his lips when he smiled. The rumble of his deep voice echoed in her chest, building to a crescendo and crumbling the wall that once stood between them.

"I'm the woman who's been in love with you for ten years," she pointed out in an unsteady whisper. "Who's crazy now?"

The glow in his eyes deepened. "I guess you could say we're both just crazy in love."

Her lips spread into in a wide smile. "I can live with that stigma."

Their breath mingled as their lips touched and clung.

Cruz tightened his hold around her, but before he deepened the kiss, he pulled back just far enough to gaze down into her eyes.

"I love you, Grace Stavenaugh. Always have, always will."

"Hey, that's my line," she protested.

"I'll let you use it when we write our vows."

"Our vows? Getting ahead of ourselves, much?" Her tone would have been playful, had it not been so breathless with excitement.

"Don't worry. I'll give you time to get used to the idea. But even way back then, I knew I wanted to marry you one day. I'm more certain of it now than ever, because I love you more than ever." Cruz crushed her to him then, kissing her in the way he had only dreamed of doing for the past ten years.

Both were oblivious to the silent alarms sent by his heart monitor. The alerts arrived at the nurse's station in staccato fashion, one after another, lighting up the alarm panel. As the couple wrapped their arms around one another and lost themselves in the other's kiss, padded feet rushed down the hall and threw the door open.

"What's wrong? Are you okay?" Shanae demanded before she cleared the isolation cubicle.

Jana was only steps behind. "Where's Grace? What's wr—?"

Shanae came to an abrupt halt, causing Jana to bump promptly into her.

"I knew it!" Shanae crowed in delight. "I knew there was something between you two! A blind woman could see it, and this girl ain't blind! I told you he was a hottie, now didn't I, Grace?"

Sheer happiness bubbled up from Grace's chest, taking the form of laughter. "That you did, my friend.

That you did."

"Should we unhook the monitor and give you two some privacy?" Jana offered sweetly.

"Oh, no," Grace insisted, her eyes dancing with mischief as she leaned back in Cruz's arms and smiled up at him. "Hand-me-down or not, I want to make certain this man's heart is in tip-top condition before I take possession."

Clearly confused, her friends exchanged a curious look. Jana mouthed the words, "Hand-me-down?"

In reply, Shanae shrugged uncertainly.

"We're clearly not needed here, so we'll just go now," Jana murmured.

"Try to take it easy on the monitor," Shanae advised.

Their snickers followed them out of the room. The couple on the couch was too busy grinning at one another to notice their retreat.

Alone once again, Cruz made a solemn correction.

"Just to make one thing perfectly clear," he told the woman in his arms. "You already possess my heart, and it's no hand-me-down. This one has only had one owner, ever. And that owner is you, Grace Stavenaugh. You've always had my heart."

THANKS FOR SPENDING THIS TIME WITH ME AT TEXAS GENERAL!

If you've enjoyed this book, please take a moment to share your rating and a brief review on Amazon and/or, Goodreads, BookBub, or the site of your choice. It may seem insignificant, but it means the world to this author! I love hearing from readers! Feel free to contact me at www.beckiwillis.com or beckiwillis.ccp@gmail.com. I'm also on Facebook and, at times, Twitter and Instagram.

ABOUT THE AUTHOR

Best-selling indie author Becki Willis loves crafting stories with believable characters in believable situations. Many of her stories stem from her own travels and from personal experiences. (No worries; she's never actually murdered anyone.)

When she's not plotting danger and adventure for her imaginary friends, Becki enjoys reading, antiquing (aka junking), unraveling a good mystery (real or imagined), dark chocolate, and a good cup of coffee. A professed history geek, Becki often weaves pieces of the past into her novels. Family is a central theme in her stories and in her life. She and her husband enjoy traveling, but believe coming home to their Texas ranch is the best part of any trip.

Becki has won numerous awards, but the real compliments come from her readers. Drop in for an e-visit anytime at beckiwillis.ccp@gmail.com, or www.beckiwillis.com.